Bayou Folk

Bayou Folk

Kate Chopin

MINT EDITIONS

Bayou Folk was first published in 1894.

This edition published by Mint Editions 2021.

ISBN 9781513271620 | E-ISBN 9781513276625

Published by Mint Editions®

 MINT
EDITIONS

minteditionbooks.com

Publishing Director: Jennifer Newens
Design & Production: Rachel Lopez Metzger
Project Manager: Micaela Clark
Typesetting: Westchester Publishing Services

Contents

A No-Account Creole

I

ONE AGREEABLE AFTERNOON IN LATE autumn two young men stood together on Canal Street, closing a conversation that had evidently begun within the club-house which they had just quitted.

"There's big money in it, Offdean," said the elder of the two. "I would n't have you touch it if there was n't. Why, they tell me Patchly's pulled a hundred thousand out of the concern a'ready."

"That may be," replied Offdean, who had been politely attentive to the words addressed to him, but whose face bore a look indicating that he was closed to conviction. He leaned back upon the clumsy stick which he carried, and continued: "It's all true, I dare say, Fitch; but a decision of that sort would mean more to me than you'd believe if I were to tell you. The beggarly twenty-five thousand's all I have, and I want to sleep with it under my pillow a couple of months at least before I drop it into a slot."

"You 'll drop it into Harding & Offdean's mill to grind out the pitiful two and a half per cent commission racket; that's what you 'll do in the end, old fellow—see if you don't."

"Perhaps I shall; but it's more than likely I shan't. We 'll talk about it when I get back. You know I'm off to north Louisiana in the morning"—

"No! What the deuce"—

"Oh, business of the firm."

"Write me from Shreveport, then; or wherever it is."

"Not so far as that. But don't expect to hear from me till you see me. I can't say when that will be."

Then they shook hands and parted. The rather portly Fitch boarded a Prytania Street car, and Mr. Wallace Offdean hurried to the bank in order to replenish his portemonnaie, which had been materially lightened at the club through the medium of unpropitious jack-pots and bobtail flushes.

He was a sure-footed fellow, this young Offdean, despite an occasional fall in slippery places. What he wanted, now that he had reached his twenty-sixth year and his inheritance, was to get his feet well planted on solid ground, and to keep his head cool and clear.

With his early youth he had had certain shadowy intentions of shaping his life on intellectual lines. That is, he wanted to; and he meant to use his faculties intelligently, which means more than is at once apparent. Above all, he would keep clear of the maelstroms of sordid work and senseless pleasure in which the average American business man may be said alternately to exist, and which reduce him, naturally, to a rather ragged condition of soul.

Offdean had done, in a temperate way, the usual things which young men do who happen to belong to good society, and are possessed of moderate means and healthy instincts. He had gone to college, had traveled a little at home and abroad, had frequented society and the clubs, and had worked in his uncle's commission-house; in all of which employments he had expended much time and a modicum of energy.

But he felt all through that he was simply in a preliminary stage of being, one that would develop later into something tangible and intelligent, as he liked to tell himself. With his patrimony of twenty-five thousand dollars came what he felt to be the turning-point in his life,—the time when it behooved him to choose a course, and to get himself into proper trim to follow it manfully and consistently.

When Messrs. Harding & Offdean determined to have some one look after what they called "a troublesome piece of land on Red River," Wallace Offdean requested to be intrusted with that special commission of land-inspector.

A shadowy, ill-defined piece of land in an unfamiliar part of his native State, might, he hoped, prove a sort of closet into which he could retire and take counsel with his inner and better self.

II

WHAT HARDING & OFFDEAN HAD called a piece of land on Red River was better known to the people of Natchitoches[1] parish as "the old Santien place."

In the days of Lucien Santien and his hundred slaves, it had been very splendid in the wealth of its thousand acres. But the war did its work, of course. Then Jules Santien was not the man to mend such damage as the war had left. His three sons were even less able than he had been to bear the weighty inheritance of debt that came to them with

---

1. Pronounced Nack-e-tosh.

the dismantled plantation; so it was a deliverance to all when Harding & Offdean, the New Orleans creditors, relieved them of the place with the responsibility and indebtedness which its ownership had entailed.

Hector, the eldest, and Grégoire, the youngest of these Santien boys, had gone each his way. Placide alone tried to keep a desultory foothold upon the land which had been his and his forefathers'. But he too was given to wandering—within a radius, however, which rarely took him so far that he could not reach the old place in an afternoon of travel, when he felt so inclined.

There were acres of open land cultivated in a slovenly fashion, but so rich that cotton and corn and weed and "cocoa-grass" grew rampant if they had only the semblance of a chance. The negro quarters were at the far end of this open stretch, and consisted of a long row of old and very crippled cabins. Directly back of these a dense wood grew, and held much mystery, and witchery of sound and shadow, and strange lights when the sun shone. Of a gin-house there was left scarcely a trace; only so much as could serve as inadequate shelter to the miserable dozen cattle that huddled within it in winter-time.

A dozen rods or more from the Red River bank stood the dwelling-house, and nowhere upon the plantation had time touched so sadly as here. The steep, black, moss-covered roof sat like an extinguisher above the eight large rooms that it covered, and had come to do its office so poorly that not more than half of these were habitable when the rain fell. Perhaps the live-oaks made too thick and close a shelter about it. The verandas were long and broad and inviting; but it was well to know that the brick pillar was crumbling away under one corner, that the railing was insecure at another, and that still another had long ago been condemned as unsafe. But that, of course, was not the corner in which Wallace Offdean sat the day following his arrival at the Santien place. This one was comparatively secure. A gloire-de-Dijon, thick-leaved and charged with huge creamy blossoms, grew and spread here like a hardy vine upon the wires that stretched from post to post. The scent of the blossoms was delicious; and the stillness that surrounded Offdean agreeably fitted his humor that asked for rest. His old host, Pierre Manton, the manager of the place, sat talking to him in a soft, rhythmic monotone; but his speech was hardly more of an interruption than the hum of the bees among the roses. He was saying:—

"If it would been me myse'f, I would nevair grumb'. W'en a chimbly breck, I take one, two de boys; we patch 'im up bes' we know how. We keep on men' de fence', firs' one place, anudder; an' if it would n' be fer dem mule' of Lacroix—*tonnerre!* I don' wan' to talk 'bout dem mule'. But me, I would n' grumb'. It's Euphrasie, hair. She say dat's all fool nonsense fer rich man lack Hardin'-Offde'n to let a piece o' lan' goin' lack dat."

"Euphrasie?" questioned Offdean, in some surprise; for he had not yet heard of any such person.

"Euphrasie, my li'le chile. Escuse me one minute," Pierre added, remembering that he was in his shirt-sleeves, and rising to reach for his coat, which hung upon a peg near by. He was a small, square man, with mild, kindly face, brown and roughened from healthy exposure. His hair hung gray and long beneath the soft felt hat that he wore. When he had seated himself, Offdean asked:—

"Where is your little child? I have n't seen her," inwardly marveling that a little child should have uttered such words of wisdom as those recorded of her.

"She yonder to Mme. Duplan on Cane River. I been kine espectin' hair sence yistiday—hair an' Placide," casting an unconscious glance down the long plantation road. "But Mme. Duplan she nevair want to let Euphrasie go. You know it's hair raise' Euphrasie sence hair po' ma die', Mr. Offde'n. She teck dat li'le chile, an' raise it, sem lack she raisin' Ninette. But it's mo' 'an a year now Euphrasie say dat's all fool nonsense to leave me livin' 'lone lack dat, wid nuttin' 'cep' dem nigger'—an' Placide once a w'ile. An' she came yair bossin'! My goodness!" The old man chuckled, "Dat's hair been writin' all dem letter' to Hardin'-Offde'n. If it would been me myse'f"—

III

PLACIDE SEEMED TO HAVE HAD a foreboding of ill from the start when he found that Euphrasie began to interest herself in the condition of the plantation. This ill feeling voiced itself partly when he told her it was none of her lookout if the place went to the dogs. "It's good enough for Joe Duplan to run things *en grand seigneur*, Euphrasie; that's w'at's spoiled you."

Placide might have done much single-handed to keep the old place in better trim, if he had wished. For there was no one more clever than he to do a hand's turn at any and every thing. He could mend a saddle or bridle while he stood whistling a tune. If a wagon required a brace or a bolt, it was nothing for him to step into a shop and turn out one as deftly as the most skilled blacksmith. Any one seeing him at work with plane and rule and chisel would have declared him a born carpenter. And as for mixing paints, and giving a fine and lasting coat to the side of a house or barn, he had not his equal in the country.

This last talent he exercised little in his native parish. It was in a neighboring one, where he spent the greater part of his time, that his fame as a painter was established. There, in the village of Orville, he owned a little shell of a house, and during odd times it was Placide's great delight to tinker at this small home, inventing daily new beauties and conveniences to add to it. Lately it had become a precious possession to him, for in the spring he was to bring Euphrasie there as his wife.

Maybe it was because of his talent, and his indifference in turning it to good, that he was often called "a no-account creole" by thriftier souls than himself. But no-account creole or not, painter, carpenter, blacksmith, and whatever else he might be at times, he was a Santien always, with the best blood in the country running in his veins. And many thought his choice had fallen in very low places when he engaged himself to marry little Euphrasie, the daughter of old Pierre Manton and a problematic mother a good deal less than nobody.

Placide might have married almost any one, too; for it was the easiest thing in the world for a girl to fall in love with him,—sometimes the hardest thing in the world not to, he was such a splendid fellow, such a careless, happy, handsome fellow. And he did not seem to mind in the least that young men who had grown up with him were lawyers now, and planters, and members of Shakespeare clubs in town. No one ever expected anything quite so humdrum as that of the Santien boys. As youngsters, all three had been the despair of the country school-master; then of the private tutor who had come to shackle them, and had failed in his design. And the state of mutiny and revolt that they had brought about at the college of Grand Coteau when their father, in a moment of weak concession to prejudice, had sent them there, is a thing yet remembered in Natchitoches.

And now Placide was going to marry Euphrasie. He could not recall the time when he had not loved her. Somehow he felt that it began the day when he was six years old, and Pierre, his father's overseer, had called him from play to come and make her acquaintance. He was permitted to hold her in his arms a moment, and it was with silent awe that he did so. She was the first white-faced baby he remembered having seen, and he straightway believed she had been sent to him as a birthday gift to be his little play-mate and friend. If he loved her, there was no great wonder; every one did, from the time she took her first dainty step, which was a brave one, too.

She was the gentlest little lady ever born in old Natchitoches parish, and the happiest and merriest. She never cried or whimpered for a hurt. Placide never did, why should she? When she wept, it was when she did what was wrong, or when he did; for that was to be a coward, she felt. When she was ten, and her mother was dead, Mme. Duplan, the Lady Bountiful of the parish, had driven across from her plantation, Les Chêniers, to old Pierre's very door, and there had gathered up this precious little maid, and carried her away, to do with as she would.

And she did with the child much as she herself had been done by. Euphrasie went to the convent soon, and was taught all gentle things, the pretty arts of manner and speech that the ladies of the "Sacred Heart" can teach so well. When she quitted them, she left a trail of love behind her; she always did.

Placide continued to see her at intervals, and to love her always. One day he told her so; he could not help it. She stood under one of the big oaks at Les Chêniers. It was midsummer time, and the tangled sunbeams had enmeshed her in a golden fret-work. When he saw her standing there in the sun's glamour, which was like a glory upon her, he trembled. He seemed to see her for the first time. He could only look at her, and wonder why her hair gleamed so, as it fell in those thick chestnut waves about her ears and neck. He had looked a thousand times into her eyes before; was it only to-day they held that sleepy, wistful light in them that invites love? How had he not seen it before? Why had he not known before that her lips were red, and cut in fine, strong curves? that her flesh was like cream? How had he not seen that she was beautiful? "Euphrasie," he said, taking her hands,—"Euphrasie, I love you!"

She looked at him with a little astonishment. "Yes; I know, Placide." She spoke with the soft intonation of the creole.

"No, you don't, Euphrasie. I did n' know myse'f how much tell jus' now."

Perhaps he did only what was natural when he asked her next if she loved him. He still held her hands. She looked thoughtfully away, unready to answer.

"Do you love anybody better?" he asked jealously. "Any one jus' as well as me?" "You know I love papa better, Placide, an' Maman Duplan jus' as well."

Yet she saw no reason why she should not be his wife when he asked her to.

Only a few months before this, Euphrasie had returned to live with her father. The step had cut her off from everything that girls of eighteen call pleasure. If it cost her one regret, no one could have guessed it. She went often to visit the Duplans, however; and Placide had gone to bring her home from Les Chêniers the very day of Offdean's arrival at the plantation.

They had traveled by rail to Natchitoches, where they found Pierre's no-top buggy awaiting them, for there was a drive of five miles to be made through the pine woods before the plantation was reached. When they were at their journey's end, and had driven some distance; up the long plantation road that led to the house in the rear, Euphrasie exclaimed:—

"W'y, there's some one on the gall'ry with papa, Placide!"

"Yes; I see."

"It looks like some one f'om town. It mus' be Mr. Gus Adams; but I don' see his horse."

"'T ain't no one f'om town that I know. It's boun' to be some one f'om the city."

"Oh, Placide, I should n' wonder if Harding & Offdean have sent some one to look after the place at las'," she exclaimed a little excitedly.

They were near enough to see that the stranger was a young man of very pleasing appearance. Without apparent reason, a chilly depression took hold of Placide.

"I tole you it was n' yo' lookout f'om the firs', Euphrasie," he said to her.

IV

WALLACE OFFDEAN REMEMBERED EUPHRASIE AT once as a young person whom he had assisted to a very high perch on his club-house balcony the previous Mardi Gras night. He had thought her pretty and attractive then, and for the space of a day or two wondered who she might be. But he had not made even so fleeting an impression upon her; seeing which, he did not refer to any former meeting when Pierre introduced them.

She took the chair which he offered her, and asked him very simply when he had come, if his journey had been pleasant, and if he had not found the road from Natchitoches in very good condition.

"Mr. Offde'n only come sence yistiday, Euphrasie," interposed Pierre. "We been talk' plenty 'bout de place, him an' me. I been tole 'im all 'bout it—*va!* An' if Mr. Offde'n want to escuse me now, I b'lieve I go he'p Placide wid dat hoss an' buggy;" and he descended the steps slowly, and walked lazily with his bent figure in the direction of the shed beneath which Placide had driven, after depositing Euphrasie at the door.

"I dare say you find it strange," began, Offdean, "that the owners of this place have neglected it so long and shamefully. But you see," he added, smiling, "the management of a plantation does n't enter into the routine of a commission merchant's business. The place has already cost them more than they hope to get from it, and naturally they have n't the wish to sink further money in it." He did not know why he was saying these things to a mere girl, but he went on: "I'm authorized to sell the plantation if I can get anything like a reasonable price for it." Euphrasie laughed in a way that made him uncomfortable, and he thought he would say no more at present,—not till he knew her better, anyhow.

"Well," she said in a very decided fashion, "I know you 'll fin' one or two persons in town who 'll begin by running down the lan' till you would n' want it as a gif', Mr. Offdean; and who will en' by offering to take it off yo' han's for the promise of a song, with the lan' as security again."

They both laughed, and Placide, who was approaching, scowled. But before he reached the steps his instinctive sense of the courtesy due to a stranger had banished the look of ill humor. His bearing was so frank and graceful, and his face such a marvel of beauty, with its dark, rich coloring and soft lines, that the well-clipped and groomed Offdean felt his astonishment to be more than half admiration when they shook hands. He knew that the Santiens had been the former owners of this plantation which he had come to look after, and naturally he expected some sort of cooperation or direct assistance from Placide in his efforts at reconstruction. But Placide proved non-committal, and exhibited an indifference and ignorance concerning the condition of affairs that savored surprisingly of affectation.

He had positively nothing to say so long as the talk touched upon matters concerning Offdean's business there. He was only a little less taciturn when more general topics were approached, and directly after supper he saddled his horse and went away. He would not wait until morning, for the moon would be rising about midnight, and he knew the road as well by night as by day. He knew just where the best fords were across the bayous, and the safest paths across the hills. He knew for a certainty whose plantations he might traverse, and whose fences he might derail. But, for that matter, he would derail what he liked, and cross where he pleased.

Euphrasie walked with him to the shed when he went for his horse. She was bewildered at his sudden determination, and wanted it explained.

"I don' like that man," he admitted frankly; "I can't stan' him. Sen' me word w'en he's gone, Euphrasie."

She was patting and rubbing the pony, which knew her well. Only their dim outlines were discernible in the thick darkness.

"You are foolish, Placide," she replied in French. "You would do better to stay and help him. No one knows the place so well as you"—

"The place isn't mine, and it's nothing to me," he answered bitterly. He took her hands and kissed them passionately, but stooping, she pressed her lips upon his forehead.

"Oh!" he exclaimed rapturously, "you do love me, Euphrasie?" His arms were holding her, and his lips brushing her hair and cheeks as they eagerly but ineffectually sought hers.

"Of co'se I love you, Placide. Ain't I going to marry you nex' spring? You foolish boy!" she replied, disengaging herself from his clasp.

When he was mounted, he stooped to say, "See yere, Euphrasie, don't have too much to do with that d—— Yankee."

"But, Placide, he is n't a—a—'d—— Yankee;' he's a Southerner, like you,—a New Orleans man."

"Oh, well, he looks like a Yankee." But Placide laughed, for he was happy since Euphrasie had kissed him, and he whistled softly as he urged his horse to a canter and disappeared in the darkness.

The girl stood awhile with clasped hands, trying to understand a little sigh that rose in her throat, and that was not one of regret. When shew regained the house, she went directly to her room, and left her father talking to Offdean in the quiet and perfumed night.

V

WHEN TWO WEEKS HAD PASSED, Offdean felt very much at home with old Pierre and his daughter, and found the business that had called him to the country so engrossing that he had given no thought to those personal questions he had hoped to solve in going there.

The old man had driven him around in the no-top buggy to show him how dismantled the fences and barns were. He could see for himself that the house was a constant menace to human life. In the evenings the three would sit out on the gallery and talk of the land and its strong points and its weak ones, till he came to know it as if it had been his own.

Of the rickety condition of the cabins he got a fair notion, for he and Euphrasie passed them almost daily on horseback, on their way to the woods. It was seldom that their appearance together did not rouse comment among the darkies who happened to be loitering about.

La Chatte, a broad black woman with ends of white wool sticking out from under her *tignon*, stood with arms *akimbo* watching them as they disappeared one day. Then she turned and said to a young woman who sat in the cabin door:—

"Dat young man, ef he want to listen to me, he gwine quit dat ar caperin' roun' Miss 'Phrasie."

The young woman in the doorway laughed, and showed her white teeth, and tossed her head, and fingered the blue beads at her throat, in a way to indicate that she was in hearty sympathy with any question that touched upon gallantry.

"Law! La Chatte, you ain' gwine hinder a gemman f'om payin' intentions to a young lady w'en he a mine to."

"Dat all I got to say," returned La Chatte, seating herself lazily and heavily on the doorstep. "Nobody don' know dem Sanchun boys bettah 'an I does. Did n' I done part raise 'em? W'at you reckon my ha'r all tu'n plumb w'ite dat-a-way ef it warn't dat Placide w'at done it?"

"How come he make yo' ha'r tu'n w'ite, La Chatte?"

"Dev'ment, pu' dev'ment, Rose. Did n' he come in dat same cabin one day, w'en he warn't no bigga 'an dat Pres'dent Hayes w'at you sees gwine 'long de road wid dat cotton sack 'crost 'im? He come an' sets down by de do', on dat same t'ree-laigged stool w'at you's a-settin' on now, wid his gun in his ban', an' he say: 'La Chatte, I wants some croquignoles, an' I wants 'em quick, too.' I 'low: 'G' 'way f'om dah, boy. Don' you see I's flutin' yo' ma's petticoat?' He say: 'La Chatte, put 'side dat ar flutin'i'on an' dat ar petticoat;' an' he cock dat gun an' p'int it to my head. 'Dar de ba'el,' he say; 'git out dat flour, git out dat butta an' dat aigs; step roun' dah, ole 'oman. Dis heah gun don' quit yo' head tell dem croquignoles is on de table, wid a w'ite table-clof an' a cup o' coffee.' Ef I goes to de ba'el, de gun's a-p'intin'. Ef I goes to de fiah, de gun's ar-p'intin'. W'en I rolls out de dough, de gun's a-p'intin'; an' him neva say nuttin', an' me a-trim'lin' like ole Uncle Noah w'en de mis'ry strike 'im."

"Lordy! w'at you reckon he do ef he tu'n roun' an' git mad wid dat young gemman f'om de city?"

"I don' reckon nuttin'; I knows w'at he gwine do,—same w'at his pa done."

"W'at his pa done, La Chatte?"

"G' 'long 'bout yo' business; you's axin' too many questions." And La Chatte arose slowly and went to gather her party-colored wash that hung drying on the jagged and irregular points of a dilapidated picket-fence.

But the darkies were mistaken in supposing that Offdean was paying attention to Euphrasie. Those little jaunts in the wood were purely of a business character. Offdean had made a contract with a neighboring mill for fencing, in exchange for a certain amount of uncut timber. He had made it his work—with the assistance of Euphrasie—to decide upon what trees he wanted felled, and to mark such for the woodman's axe.

If they sometimes forgot what they had gone into the woods for, it was because there was so much to talk about and to laugh about. Often, when Offdean had blazed a tree with the sharp hatchet which he carried at his pommel, and had further discharged his duty by calling it "a fine piece of timber," they would sit upon some fallen and decaying trunk, maybe to listen to a chorus of mocking-birds above their heads, or to exchange confidences, as young people will.

Euphrasie thought she had never heard any one talk quite so pleasantly as Offdean did. She could not decide whether it was his manner or the tone of his voice, or the earnest glance of his dark and deep-set blue eyes, that gave such meaning to everything he said; for she found herself afterward thinking of his every word.

One afternoon it rained in torrents, and Rose was forced to drag buckets and tubs into Offdean's room to catch the streams that threatened to flood it. Euphrasie said she was glad of it; now he could see for himself.

And when he had seen for himself, he went to join her out on a corner of the gallery, where she stood with a cloak around her, close up against the house. He leaned against the house, too, and they stood thus together, gazing upon as desolate a scene as it is easy to imagine.

The whole landscape was gray, seen through the driving rain. Far away the dreary cabins seemed to sink and sink to earth in abject misery. Above their heads the live-oak branches were beating with sad monotony against the blackened roof. Great pools of water had formed in the yard, which was deserted by every living thing; for the little darkies had scampered away to their cabins, the dogs had run to their kennels, and the hens were puffing big with wretchedness under the scanty shelter of a fallen wagon-body.

Certainly a situation to make a young man groan with ennui, if he is used to his daily stroll on Canal Street, and pleasant afternoons at the club. But Offdean thought it delightful. He only wondered that he had never known, or some one had never told him, how charming a place an old, dismantled plantation can be—when it rains. But as well as he liked it, he could not linger there forever. Business called him back to New Orleans, and after a few days he went away.

The interest which he felt in the improvement of this plantation was of so deep a nature, however, that he found himself thinking of it constantly. He wondered if the timber had all been felled, and how the fencing was coming on. So great was his desire to know such things that much correspondence was required between himself and Euphrasie, and he watched eagerly for those letters that told him of her trials and vexations with carpenters, bricklayers, and shingle—bearers. But in the midst of it, Offdean suddenly lost interest in the progress of work on the plantation. Singularly enough, it happened simultaneously with the arrival of a letter from Euphrasie which announced in a modest postscript that she was going down to the city with the Duplans for Mardi Gras.

VI

When Offdean learned that Euphrasie was coming to New Orleans, he was delighted to think he would have an opportunity to make some return for the hospitality which he had received from her father. He decided at once that she must see everything: day processions and night parades, balls and tableaux, operas and plays. He would arrange for it all, and he went to the length of begging to be relieved of certain duties that had been assigned him at the club, in order that he might feel himself perfectly free to do so.

The evening following Euphrasie's arrival, Offdean hastened to call upon her, away down on Esplanade Street. She and the Duplans were staying there with old Mme. Carantelle, Mrs. Duplan's mother, a delightfully conservative old lady who had not "crossed Canal Street" for many years.

He found a number of people gathered in the long high-ceiled drawing-room,—young people and old people, all talking French, and some talking louder than they would have done if Madame Carantelle had not been so very deaf.

When Offdean entered, the old lady was greeting some one who had come in just before him. It was Placide, and she was calling him Grégoire, and wanting to know how the crops were up on Red River. She met every one from the country with this stereotyped inquiry, which placed her at once on the agreeable and easy footing she liked.

Somehow Offdean had not counted on finding Euphrasie so well provided with entertainment, and he spent much of the evening in trying to persuade himself that the fact was a pleasing one in itself. But he wondered why Placide was with her, and sat so persistently beside her, and danced so repeatedly with her when Mrs. Duplan played upon the piano. Then he could not see by what right these young creoles had already arranged for the Proteus ball, and every other entertainment that he had meant to provide for her.

He went away without having had a word alone with the girl whom he had gone to see. The evening had proved a failure. He did not go to the club as usual, but went to his rooms in a mood which inclined him to read a few pages from a stoic philosopher whom he sometimes affected. But the words of wisdom that had often before helped him over disagreeable places left no impress to-night. They were powerless to banish from his thoughts the look of a pair of brown eyes, or to drown the tones of a girl's voice that kept singing in his soul.

Placide was not very well acquainted with the city; but that made no difference to him so long as he was at Euphrasie's side. His brother Hector, who lived in some obscure corner of the town, would willingly have made his knowledge a more intimate one; but Placide did not choose to learn the lessons that Hector was ready to teach. He asked nothing better than to walk with Euphrasie along the streets, holding her parasol at an agreeable angle over her pretty head, or to sit beside her in the evening at the play, sharing her frank delight.

When the night of the Mardi Gras ball came, he felt like a lost spirit during the hours he was forced to remain away from her. He stood in the dense crowd on the street gazing up at her, where she sat on the club-house balcony amid a bevy of gayly dressed women. It was not easy to distinguish her, but he could think of no more agreeable occupation than to stand down there on the street trying to do so.

She seemed during all this pleasant time to be entirely his own, too. It made him very fierce to think of the possibility of her not being entirely his own. But he had no cause whatever to think this. She had grown conscious and thoughtful of late about him and their relationship. She often communed with herself, and as a result tried to act toward him as an engaged girl would toward her fiancé. Yet a wistful look came sometimes into the brown eyes when she walked the streets with Placide, and eagerly scanned the faces of passers-by.

Offdean had written her a note, very studied, very formal, asking to see her a certain day and hour, to consult about matters on the plantation, saying he had found it so difficult to obtain a word with her, that he was forced to adopt this means, which he trusted would not be offensive.

This seemed perfectly right to Euphrasie. She agreed to see him one afternoon—the day before leaving town—in the long, stately drawing-room, quite alone.

It was a sleepy day, too warm for the season. Gusts of moist air were sweeping lazily through the long corridors, rattling the slats of the half-closed green shutters, and bringing a delicious perfume from the courtyard where old Chariot was watering the spreading palms and brilliant parterres. A group of little children had stood awhile quarreling noisily under the windows, but had moved on down the street and left quietness reigning.

Offdean had not long to wait before Euphrasie came to him. She had lost some of that ease which had marked her manner during their first acquaintance. Now, when she seated herself before him, she showed a disposition to plunge at once into the subject that had brought him there. He was willing enough that it should play some rôle, since it had been his pretext for coming; but he soon dismissed it, and with it much restraint that had held him till now. He simply looked into her eyes, with a gaze that made her shiver a little, and began to complain because she was going away next day and he had seen nothing of her; because he had wanted to do so many things when she came—why had she not let him?

"You fo'get I'm no stranger here," she told him. "I know many people.

I've been coming so often with Mme. Duplan. I wanted to see mo' of you, Mr. Offdean"—

"Then you ought to have managed it; you could have done so. It's—it's aggravating," he said, far more bitterly than the subject warranted, "when a man has so set his heart upon something."

"But it was n' anything ver' important," she interposed; and they both laughed, and got safely over a situation that would soon have been strained, if not critical.

Waves of happiness were sweeping through the soul and body of the girl as she sat there in the drowsy afternoon near the man whom she loved. It mattered not what they talked about, or whether they talked at all. They were both scintillant with feeling. If Offdean had taken Euphrasie's hands in his and leaned forward and kissed her lips, it would have seemed to both only the rational outcome of things that stirred them. But he did not do this. He knew now that overwhelming passion was taking possession of him. He had not to heap more coals upon the fire; on the contrary, it was a moment to put on the brakes, and he was a young gentleman able to do this when circumstances required.

However, he held her hand longer than he needed to when he bade her good-by. For he got entangled in explaining why he should have to go back to the plantation to see how matters stood there, and he dropped her hand only when the rambling speech was ended.

He left her sitting by the window in a big brocaded armchair. She drew the lace curtain aside to watch him pass in the street. He lifted his hat and smiled when he saw her. Any other man she knew would have done the same thing, but this simple act caused the blood to surge to her cheeks. She let the curtain drop, and sat there like one dreaming. Her eyes, intense with the unnatural light that glowed in them, looked steadily into vacancy, and her lips stayed parted in the half-smile that did not want to leave them.

Placide found her thus, a good while afterward, when he came in, full of bustle, with theatre tickets in his pocket for the last night. She started up, and went eagerly to meet him.

"W'ere have you been, Placide?" she asked with unsteady voice, placing her hands on his shoulders with a freedom that was new and strange to him.

He appeared to her suddenly as a refuge from something, she did not know what, and she rested her hot cheek against his breast. This made him mad, and he lifted her face and kissed her passionately upon the lips.

She crept from his arms after that, and went away to her room, and locked herself in. Her poor little inexperienced soul was torn and sore. She knelt down beside her bed, and sobbed a little and prayed a little. She felt that she had sinned, she did not know exactly in what; but a fine nature warned her that it was in Placide's kiss.

VII

THE SPRING CAME EARLY IN Orville, and so subtly that no one could tell exactly when it began. But one morning the roses were so luscious in Placide's sunny parterres, the peas and bean-vines and borders of strawberries so rank in his trim vegetable patches, that he called out lustily, "No mo' winta, Judge!" to the staid Judge Blount, who went ambling by on his gray pony.

"There's right smart o' folks don't know it, Santien," responded the judge, with occult meaning that might be applied to certain indebted clients back on the bayou who had not broken land yet. Ten minutes later the judge observed sententiously, and apropos of nothing, to a group that stood waiting for the post-office to open:—

"I see Santien's got that noo fence o' his painted. And a pretty piece o' work it is," he added reflectively.

"Look lack Placide goin' pent mo' 'an de fence," sagaciously snickered 'Tit-Edouard, a strolling *maigre-échine* of indefinite occupation. "I seen 'im, me, pesterin' wid all kine o' pent on a piece o' bo'd yistiday."

"I knows he gwine paint mo' 'an de fence," emphatically announced Uncle Abner, in a tone that carried conviction.

"He gwine paint de house; dat what he gwine do. Did n' Marse Luke Williams orda de paints? An' did n' I done kyar' 'em up dah myse'f?"

Seeing the deference with which this positive piece of knowledge was received, the judge coolly changed the subject by announcing that Luke Williams's Durham bull had broken a leg the night before in Luke's new pasture ditch,—a piece of news that fell among his hearers with telling, if paralytic effect.

But most people wanted to see for themselves these astonishing things that Placide was doing. And the young ladies of the village strolled slowly by of afternoons in couples and arm in arm. If Placide happened to see them, he would leave his work to hand them a fine rose or a bunch of geraniums over the dazzling white fence. But if it chanced to be 'Tit-Edouard or Luke Williams, or any of the young men of Orville, he pretended not to see them, or to hear the ingratiating cough that accompanied their lingering footsteps.

In his eagerness to have his home sweet and attractive for Euphrasie's coming, Placide had gone less frequently than ever before up to Natchitoches. He worked and whistled and sang until the yearning for the girl's presence became a driving need; then he would put away his tools and mount his horse as the day was closing, and away he would go across bayous and hills and fields until he was with her again. She had never seemed to Placide so lovable as she was then. She had grown more womanly and thoughtful. Her cheek had lost much of its color, and the light in her eyes flashed less often. But her manner had gained a something of pathetic tenderness toward her lover that moved him with an intoxicating happiness. He could hardly wait with patience for that day in early April which would see the fulfillment of his lifelong hopes.

After Euphrasie's departure from New Orleans, Offdean told himself honestly that he loved the girl. But being yet unsettled in life, he felt it was no time to think of marrying, and, like the worldly-wise young gentleman that he was, resolved to forget the little Natchitoches girl. He knew it would be an affair of some difficulty, but not an impossible thing, so he set about forgetting her.

The effort made him singularly irascible. At the office he was gloomy and taciturn; at the club he was a bear. A few young ladies whom he called upon were astonished and distressed at the cynical views of life which he had so suddenly adopted.

When he had endured a week or more of such humor, and inflicted it upon others, he abruptly changed his tactics. He decided not to fight against his love for Euphrasie. He would not marry her,—certainly not; but he would let himself love her to his heart's bent, until that love should die a natural death, and not a violent one as he had designed. He abandoned himself completely to his passion, and dreamed of the girl by day and thought of her by night. How delicious had been the scent of her hair, the warmth of her breath, the nearness of her body, that rainy day when they stood close together upon the veranda! He recalled the glance of her honest, beautiful eyes, that told him things which made his heart beat fast now when he thought of them. And then her voice! Was there another like it when she laughed or when she talked!

Was there another woman in the world possessed of so alluring a charm as this one he loved!

He was not bearish now, with these sweet thoughts crowding his brain and thrilling his blood; but he sighed deeply, and worked languidly, and enjoyed himself listlessly.

One day he sat in his room puffing the air thick with sighs and smoke, when a thought came suddenly to him—an inspiration, a very message from heaven, to judge from the cry of joy with which he greeted it. He sent his cigar whirling through the window, over the stone paving of the street, and he let his head fall down upon his arms, folded upon the table.

It had happened to him, as it does to many, that the solution of a vexed question flashed upon him when he was hoping least for it. He positively laughed aloud, and somewhat hysterically. In the space of a moment he saw the whole delicious future which a kind fate had mapped out for him: those rich acres upon the Red River his own, bought and embellished with his inheritance; and Euphrasie, whom he loved, his wife and companion throughout a life such as he knew now he had craved for,—a life that, imposing bodily activity, admits the intellectual repose in which thought unfolds.

Wallace Offdean was like one to whom a divinity had revealed his vocation in life,—no less a divinity because it was love. If doubts assailed him of Euphrasie's consent, they were soon stilled. For had they not spoken over and over to each other the mute and subtle language of reciprocal love—out under the forest trees, and in the quiet night-time on the plantation when the stars shone? And never so plainly as in the stately old drawing-room down on, Esplanade Street. Surely no other speech was needed then, save such as their eyes told. Oh, he knew that she loved him; he was sure of it! The knowledge made him all the more eager now to hasten to her, to tell her that he wanted her for his very own.

VIII

If Offdean had stopped in Natchitoches on his way to the plantation, he would have heard something there to astonish him, to say the very least; for the whole town was talking of Euphrasie's wedding, which was to take place in a few days. But he did not linger. After securing a horse at the stable, he pushed on with all the speed of which the animal was capable, and only in such company as his eager thoughts afforded him.

The plantation was very quiet, with that stillness which broods over broad, clean acres that furnish no refuge for so much as a bird that sings. The negroes were scattered about the fields at work, with hoe and plow, under the sun, and old Pierre, on his horse, was far off in the midst of them.

Placide had arrived in the morning, after traveling all night, and had gone to his room for an hour or two of rest. He had drawn the lounge close up to the window to get what air he might through the closed shutters. He was just beginning to doze when he heard Euphrasie's light footsteps approaching. She stopped and seated herself so near that he could have touched her if he had but reached out his hand. Her nearness banished all desire to sleep, and he lay there content to rest his limbs and think of her.

The portion of the gallery on which Euphrasie sat was facing the river, and away from the road by which Offdean had reached the house. After fastening his horse, he mounted the steps, and traversed the broad hall that intersected the house from end to end, and that was open wide. He found Euphrasie engaged upon a piece of sewing. She was hardly aware of his presence before he had seated himself beside her.

She could not spesik. She only looked at him with frightened eyes, as if his presence were that of some disembodied spirit.

"Are you not glad that I have come?" he asked her. "Have I made a mistake in coming?" He was gazing into her eyes, seeking to read the meaning of their new, and strange expression.

"Am I glad?" she faltered. "I don' know. W'at has that to do? You've come to see the work, of co'se. It's—it's only half done, Mr. Offdean. They would n' listen to me or to papa, an' you did n' seem to care."

"I have n't come to see the work," he said, with a smile of love and confidence. "I am here only to see you,—to say how much I want you, and need you—to tell you how I love you."

She rose, half choking with words she could not utter. But he seized her hands and held her there.

"The plantation is mine, Euphrasie,—or it will be when you say that you will be my wife," he went on excitedly. "I know that you love me"—

"I do not!" she exclaimed wildly. "W'at do you mean? How do you dare," she gasped, "to say such things w'en you know that in two days I shall be married to Placide" The last was said in a whisper; it was like a wail.

"Married to Placide!" he echoed, as if striving to understand,—to grasp some part of his own stupendous folly and blindness. "I knew nothing of it," he said hoarsely. "Married to Placide! I would never have spoken to you as I did, if I had known. You believe me, I hope? Please say that you forgive me."

He spoke with long silences between his utterances.

"Oh, there is n' anything to fo'give. You've only made a mistake. Please leave me, Mr. Offdean. Papa is out in the fiel', I think, if you would like to speak with him. Placide is somew'ere on the place."

"I shall mount my horse and go see what work has been done," said Offdean, rising. An unusual pallor had overspread his face, and his mouth was drawn with suppressed pain. "I must turn my fool's errand to some practical good," he added, with a sad attempt at playfulness; and with no further word he walked quickly away.

She listened to his going. Then all the wretchedness of the past months, together with the sharp distress of the moment, voiced itself in a sob: "O God—O my God, he'p me!"

But she could not stay out there in the broad day for any chance comer to look upon her uncovered sorrow.

Placide heard her rise and go to her room. When he had heard the key turn in the lock, he got up, and with quiet deliberation prepared to go out. He drew on his boots, then his coat. He took his pistol from the dressing-bureau, where he had placed it a while before, and after examining its chambers carefully, thrust it into his pocket. He had certain work to do with the weapon before night. But for Euphrasie's presence he might have accomplished it very surely a moment ago, when the hound—as he called him—stood outside his window. He did not wish her to know anything of his movements, and he left his room as quietly as possible, and mounted his horse, as Offdean had done.

"La Chatte," called Placide to the old woman, who stood in her yard at the wash-tub, "w'ich way did that man go?"

"W'at man dat? I is n' studyin' 'bout no mans; I got 'nough to do wid dis heah washin'. 'Fo' God, I don' know w'at man you's talkin' 'bout"—

"La Chatte, w'ich way did that man go? Quick, now!" with the deliberate tone and glance that had always quelled her.

"Ef you 's talkin' 'bout dat Noo Orleans man, I could 'a' tole you dat. He done tuck de road to de cocoa-patch," plunging her black arms into the tub with unnecessary energy and disturbance.

"That's enough. I know now he's gone into the woods. You always was a liar, La Chatte."

"Dat his own lookout, de smoove-tongue' raskil," soliloquized the woman a moment later. "I done said he did n' have no call to come heah, caperin' roun' Miss 'Phrasie."

Placide was possessed by only one thought, which was a want as well,—to put an end to this man who had come between him and his love. It was the same brute passion that drives the beast to slay when he sees the object of his own desire laid hold of by another.

He had heard Euphrasie tell the man she did not love him, but what of that? Had he not heard her sobs, and guessed what her distress was? It needed no very flexible mind to guess as much, when a hundred signs besides, unheeded before, came surging to his memory. Jealousy held him, and rage and despair.

Offdean, as he rode along under the trees in apathetic despondency, heard some one approaching him on horseback, and turned aside to make room in the narrow pathway.

It was not a moment for punctilious scruples, and Placide had not been hindered by such from sending a bullet into the back of his rival. The only thing that stayed him was that Offdean must know why he had to die.

"Mr. Offdean," Placide said, reining his horse with one hand, while he held his pistol openly in the other, "I was in my room 'w'ile ago, and yeared w'at you said to Euphrasie. I would 'a' killed you then if she had n' been 'longside o' you. I could 'a' killed you jus' now w'en I come up behine you."

"Well, why did n't you?" asked Offdean, meanwhile gathering his faculties to think how he had best deal with this madman.

"Because I wanted you to know who done it, an' w'at he done it for."

"Mr. Santien, I suppose to a person in your frame of mind it will make no difference to know that I'm unarmed. But if you make any attempt upon my life, I shall certainly defend myself as best I can."

"Defen' yo'se'f, then."

"You must be mad," said Offdean, quickly, and looking straight into Placide's eyes, "to want to soil your happiness with murder. I thought a creole knew better than that how to love a woman."

"By—! are you goin' to learn me how to love a woman?"

"No, Placide," said Offdean eagerly, as they rode slowly along; "your own honor is going to tell you that. The way to love a woman is to think first of her happiness. If you love Euphrasie, you must go to her clean. I love her myself enough to want you to do that. I shall leave this place to-morrow; you will never see me again if I can help it. Is n't that enough for you? I'm going to turn here and leave you. Shoot me in the back if you like; but I know you won't." And Offdean held out his hand.

"I don' want to shake han's with you," said Placide sulkily. "Go 'way f'om me." He stayed motionless watching Offdean ride away. He looked at the pistol in his hand, and replaced it slowly in his pocket; then he removed the broad felt hat which he wore, and wiped away the moisture that had gathered upon his forehead.

Offdean's words had touched some chord within him and made it vibrant; but they made him hate the man no less.

"The way to love a woman is to think firs' of her happiness," he muttered reflectively. "He thought a creole knew how to love. Does he reckon he's goin' to learn a creole how to love?"

His face was white and set with despair now. The rage had all left it as he rode deeper on into the wood.

IX

OFFDEAN ROSE EARLY, WISHING TO take the morning train to the city. But he was not before Euphrasie, whom he found in the large hall arranging the breakfast-table. Old Pierre was there too, walking slowly about with hands folded behind him, and with bowed head.

A restraint hung upon all of them, and the girl turned to her father and asked him if Placide were up, seemingly for want of something to say. The old man fell heavily into a chair, and gazed upon her in the deepest distress.

"Oh, my po' li'le Euphrasie! my po' li'le chile! Mr. Offde'n, you ain't no stranger."

"*Bon Dieu!* Papa!" cried the girl sharply, seized with a vague terror. She quitted her occupation at the table, and stood in nervous apprehension of what might follow.

"I yaired people say Placide was one no-'count creole. I nevair want to believe dat, me. Now I know dat's true. Mr. Offde'n, you ain't no stranger, you."

Offdean was gazing upon the old man in amazement.

"In de night," Pierre continued, "I yaired some noise on de winder. I go open, an' dere Placide, standin' wid his big boot' on, an' his w'ip w'at he knocked wid on de winder, an' his hoss all saddle'. Oh, my po' li'le chile! He say, 'Pierre, I yaired say Mr. Luke William' want his house pent down in Orville. I reckon I go git de job befo' somebody else teck it.' I say, 'You come straight back, Placide?' He say, 'Don' look fer me.' An' w'en I ax 'im w'at I goin' tell to my li'le chile, he say, 'Tell Euphrasie Placide know better 'an anybody livin' w'at goin' make her happy.' An' he start 'way; den he come back an' say, 'Tell dat man'—I don' know who he was talk' 'bout—k tell 'im he ain't goin' learn nuttin' to a creole.' *Mon Dieu! Mon Dieu!* I don' know w'at all dat mean."

He was holding the half-fainting Euphrasie in his arms, and stroking her hair.

"I always yaired say he was one no-'count creole. I nevair want to believe dat."

"Don't—don't say that again, papa," she whisperingly entreated, speaking in French. "Placide has saved me!"

"He has save' you f'om w'at, Euphrasie?" asked her father, in dazed astonishment.

"From sin," she replied to him under her breath.

"I don' know w'at all dat mean," the old man muttered, bewildered, as he arose and walked out on the gallery.

Offdean had taken coffee in his room, and would not wait for breakfast. When he went to bid Euphrasie good-by, she sat beside the table with her head bowed upon her arm.

He took her hand and said good-by to her, but she did not look up.

"Euphrasie," he asked eagerly, "I may come back? Say that I may—after a while."

She gave him no answer, and he leaned down and pressed his cheek caressingly and entreatingly against her soft thick hair.

"May I, Euphrasie?" he begged. "So long as you do not tell me no, I shall come back, dearest one."

She still made him no reply, but she did not tell him no.

So he kissed her hand and her cheek,—what he could touch of it, that peeped out from her folded arm,—and went away.

An hour later, when Offdean passed through Natchitoches, the old town was already ringing with the startling news that Placide had been dismissed by his *fiancée*, and the wedding was off, information which the young creole was taking the trouble to scatter broadcast as he went.

In and Out of Old Natchitoches

Precisely at eight o'clock every morning except Saturdays and Sundays, Mademoiselle Suzanne St. Denys Godolph would cross the railroad trestle that spanned Bayou Boispourri. She might have crossed in the flat which Mr. Alphonse Laballière kept for his own convenience; but the method was slow and unreliable; so, every morning at eight, Mademoiselle St. Denys Godolph crossed the trestle.

She taught public school in a picturesque little white frame structure that stood upon Mr. Laballière's land, and hung upon the very brink of the bayou.

Laballière himself was comparatively a new-comer in the parish. It was barely six months since he decided one day to leave the sugar and rice to his brother Alcée, who had a talent for their cultivation, and to try his hand at cotton-planting. That was why he was up in Natchitoches parish on a piece of rich, high, Cane River land, knocking into shape a tumbled-down plantation that he had bought for next to nothing.

He had often during his perambulations observed the trim, graceful figure stepping cautiously over the ties, and had sometimes shivered for its safety. He always exchanged a greeting with the girl, and once threw a plank over a muddy pool for her to step upon. He caught but glimpses of her features, for she wore an enormous sun-bonnet to shield her complexion, that seemed marvelously fair; while loosely—fitting leather gloves protected her hands. He knew she was the school-teacher, and also that she was the daughter of that very pig-headed old Madame St. Denys Godolph who was hoarding her barren acres across the bayou as a miser hoards gold. Starving over them, some people said. But that was nonsense; nobody starves on a Louisiana plantation, unless it be with suicidal intent.

These things he knew, but he did not know why Mademoiselle St. Denys Godolph always answered his salutation with an air of chilling hauteur that would easily have paralyzed a less sanguine man.

The reason was that Suzanne, like every one else, had heard the stories that were going the rounds about him. People said he was entirely too much at home with the free mulattoes.[1] It seems a dreadful

---

1. A term still applied in Louisiana to mulattoes who were never in slavery, and whose families in most instances were themselves slave owners.

KATE CHOPIN

thing to say, and it would be a shocking thing to think of a Laballière; but it was n't true.

When Laballière took possession of his land, he found the plantation-house occupied by one Giestin and his swarming family. It was past reckoning how long the free mulatto and his people had been there. The house was a six-room, long, shambling affair, shrinking together from decrepitude. There was not an entire pane of glass in the structure; and the Turkey-red curtains flapped in and out of the broken apertures. But there is no need to dwell upon details; it was wholly unfit to serve as a civilized human habitation; and Alphonse Laballière would no sooner have disturbed its contented occupants than he would have scattered a family of partridges nesting in a corner of his field. He established himself with a few belongings in the best cabin he could find on the place, and, without further ado, proceeded to supervise the building of house, of gin, of this, that, and the other, and to look into the hundred details that go to set a neglected plantation in good working order. He took his meals at the free mulatto's, quite apart from the family, of course; and they attended, not too skillfully, to his few domestic wants.

Some loafer whom he had snubbed remarked one day in town that Laballière had more use for a free mulatto than he had for a white man. It was a sort of catching thing to say, and suggestive, and was repeated with the inevitable embellishments.

One morning when Laballière sat eating his solitary breakfast, and being waited upon by the queenly Madame Giestin and a brace of her weazened boys, Giestin himself came into the room. He was about half the size of his wife, puny and timid. He stood beside the table, twirling his felt hat aimlessly and balancing himself insecurely on his high-pointed boot-heels.

"Mr. Laballière," he said, "I reckon I tell you; it's betta you git shed o' me en' my fambly. Jis like you want, yas."

"What in the name of common sense are you talking about?" asked Laballière, looking up abstractedly from his New Orleans paper. Giestin wriggled uncomfortably.

"It 's 'heap o' story goin' roun' 'bout you, if you want b'lieve me." And he snickered and looked at his wife, who thrust the end of her shawl into her mouth and walked from the room with a tread like the Empress Eugenie's, in that elegant woman's palmiest days.

"Stories!" echoed Laballière, his face the picture of astonishment. "Who—where—what stories?"

"Yon'a in town en' all about. It's heap o' tale goin' roun', yas. They say how come you mighty fon' o' mulatta. You done shoshiate wid de mulatta down yon'a on de suga plantation, tell you can't res' lessen it's mulatta roun' you."

Laballière had a distressingly quick temper. His fist, which was a strong one, came down upon the wobbling table with a crash that sent half of Madame Giestin's crockery bouncing and crashing to the floor. He swore an oath that sent Madame Giestin and her father and grandmother, who were all listening in the next room, into suppressed convulsions of mirth.

"Oh, ho! so I'm not to associate with whom I please in Natchitoches parish. We'll see about that. Draw up your chair, Giestin. Call your wife and your grandmother and the rest of the tribe, and we'll breakfast together. By thunder! if I want to hobnob with mulattoes, or negroes or Choctaw Indians or South Sea savages, whose business is it but my own?"

"I don' know, me. It's jis like I tell you, Mr. Laballière," and Giestin selected a huge key from an assortment that hung against the wall, and left the room.

A half hour later, Laballière had not yet recovered his senses. He appeared suddenly at the door of the schoolhouse, holding by the shoulder one of Giestin's boys. Mademoiselle St. Denys Godolph stood at the opposite extremity of the room. Her sun-bonnet hung upon the wall, now, so Laballière could have seen how charming she was, had he not at the moment been blinded by stupidity. Her blue eyes that were fringed with dark lashes reflected astonishment at seeing him there. Her hair was dark like her lashes, and waved softly about her smooth, white forehead.

"Mademoiselle," began Laballière at once, "I have taken the liberty of bringing a new pupil to you."

Mademoiselle St. Denys Godolph paled suddenly and her voice was unsteady when she replied:—

"You are too considerate, Monsieur. Will you be so kine to give me the name of the scholar whom you desire to int'oduce into this school?" She knew it as well as he.

"What's your name, youngster? Out with it!" cried Laballière, striving to shake the little free mulatto into speech; but he stayed as dumb as a mummy.

"His name is André Giestin. You know him. He is the son"—

"Then, Monsieur," she interrupted, "permit me to remine you that you have made a se'ious mistake. This is not a school conducted fo' the education of the colored population. You will have to go elsew'ere with yo' protégé."

"I shall leave my protégé right here, Mademoiselle, and I trust you'll give him the same kind attention you seem to accord to the others;" saying which Laballière bowed himself out of her presence. The little Giestin, left to his own devices, took only the time to give a quick, wary glance round the room, and the next instant he bounded through the open door, as the nimblest of four-footed creatures might have done.

Mademoiselle St. Denys Godolph conducted school during the hours that remained, with a deliberate calmness that would have seemed ominous to her pupils, had they been better versed in the ways of young women. When the hour for dismissal came, she rapped upon the table to demand attention.

"Chil'ren," she began, assuming a resigned and dignified mien, "you all have been witness to-day of the insult that has been offered to yo' teacher by the person upon whose lan' this schoolhouse stan's. I have nothing further to say on that subjec'. I only shall add that to-morrow yo' teacher shall sen' the key of this schoolhouse, together with her resignation, to the gentlemen who compose the school-boa'd." There followed visible disturbance among the young people.

"I ketch that li'le m'latta, I make 'im see sight', yas," screamed one.

"Nothing of the kine, Mathurin, you mus' take no such step, if only out of consideration fo' my wishes. The person who has offered the affront I consider beneath my notice. André, on the other han', is a chile of good impulse, an' by no means to blame. As you all perceive, he has shown mo' taste and judgment than those above him, f'om whom we might have espected good breeding, at least."

She kissed them all, the little boys and the little girls, and had a kind word for each. "*Et toi, mon petit Numa, j'espère q'un autre*"—She could not finish the sentence, for little Numa, her favorite, to whom she had never been able to impart the first word of English, was blubbering at a turn of affairs which he had only miserably guessed at.

She locked the schoolhouse door and walked away towards the bridge. By the time she reached it, the little 'Cadians had already disappeared like rabbits, down the road and through and over the fences.

Mademoiselle St. Denys Godolph did not cross the trestle the following day, nor the next nor the next. Laballière watched for her; for his big heart was already sore and filled with shame. But more, it stung him with remorse to realize that he had been the stupid instrument in taking the bread, as it were, from the mouth of Mademoiselle St. Denys Godolph.

He recalled how unflinchingly and haughtily her blue eyes had challenged his own. Her sweetness and charm came back to him and he dwelt upon them and exaggerated them, till no Venus, so far unearthed, could in any way approach Mademoiselle St. Denys Godolph. He would have liked to exterminate the Giestin family, from the great-grandmother down to the babe unborn.

Perhaps Giesten suspected this unfavorable attitude, for one morning he piled his whole family and all his effects into wagons, and went away; over into that part of the parish known as *l'Isle des Mulâtres*.

Laballière's really chivalrous nature told him, beside, that he owed an apology, at least, to the young lady who had taken his whim so seriously. So he crossed the bayou one day and penetrated into the wilds where Madame St. Denys Godolph ruled.

An alluring little romance formed in his mind as he went; he fancied how easily it might follow the apology. He was almost in love with Mademoiselle St. Denys Godolph when he quitted his plantation. By the time he had reached hers, he was wholly so.

He was met by Madame mere, a sweet-eyed, faded woman, upon whom old age had fallen too hurriedly to completely efface all traces of youth. But the house was old beyond question; decay had eaten slowly to the heart of it during the hours, the days, and years that it had been standing.

"I have come to see your daughter, madame," began Laballière, all too bluntly; for there is no denying he was blunt.

"Mademoiselle St. Denys Godolph is not presently at home, sir," madame replied. "She is at the time in New Orleans. She fills there a place of high trus' an' employment, Monsieur Laballière."

WHEN SUZANNE HAD EVER THOUGHT of New Orleans, it was always in connection with Hector Santien, because he was the only soul she knew who dwelt there. He had had no share in obtaining for her the position she had secured with one of the leading dry-goods firms; yet it was to him she addressed herself when her arrangements to leave home were completed.

He did not wait for her train to reach the city, but crossed the river and met her at Gretna. The first thing he did was to kiss her, as he had done eight years before when he left Natchitoches parish. An hour later he would no more have thought of kissing Suzanne than he would have tendered an embrace to the Empress of China. For by that time he had realized that she was no longer twelve nor he twenty-four.

She could hardly believe the man who met her to be the Hector of old. His black hair was dashed with gray on the temples; he wore a short, parted beard and a small moustache that curled. From the crown of his glossy silk hat down to his trimly-gaitered feet, his attire was faultless. Suzanne knew her Natchitoches, and she had been to Shreveport and even penetrated as far as Marshall, Texas, but in all her travels she had never met a man to equal Hector in the elegance of his mien.

They entered a cab, and seemed to drive for an interminable time through the streets, mostly over cobble-stones that rendered conversation difficult. Nevertheless he talked incessantly, while she peered from the windows to catch what glimpses she could, through the night, of that New Orleans of which she had heard so much. The sounds were bewildering; so were the lights, that were uneven, too, serving to make the patches of alternating gloom more mysterious.

She had not thought of asking him where he was taking her. And it was only after they crossed Canal and had penetrated some distance into Royal Street, that he told her. He was taking her to a friend of his, the dearest little woman in town. That was Maman Chavan, who was going to board and lodge her for a ridiculously small consideration.

Maman Chavan lived within comfortable walking distance of Canal Street, on one of those narrow, intersecting streets between Royal and Chartres. Her house was a tiny, single-story one, with overhanging gable, heavily shuttered door and windows and three wooden steps leading down to the banquette. A small garden flanked it on one side, quite screened from outside view by a high fence, over which appeared the tops of orange trees and other luxuriant shrubbery.

She was waiting for them—a lovable, fresh-looking, white-haired, black-eyed, small, fat little body, dressed all in black. She understood no English; which made no difference. Suzanne and Hector spoke but French to each other.

Hector did not tarry a moment longer than was needed to place his young friend and charge in the older woman's care. He would not even stay to take a bite of supper with them. Maman Chavan watched him as he hurried down the steps and out into the gloom. Then she said to Suzanne: "That man is an angel, Mademoiselle, *un ange du bon Dieu*."

"Women, my dear Maman Chavan, you know how it is with me in regard to women. I have drawn a circle round my heart, so—at pretty long range, mind you—and there is not one who gets through it, or over it or under it."

"*Blagueur, va!*" laughed Maman Chavan, replenishing her glass from the bottle of sauterne.

It was Sunday morning. They were breakfasting together on the pleasant side gallery that led by a single step down to the garden. Hector came every Sunday morning, an hour or so before noon, to breakfast with them. He always brought a bottle of sauterne, a paté, or a mess of artichokes or some tempting bit of *charcuterie*. Sometimes he had to wait till the two women returned from hearing mass at the cathedral. He did not go to mass himself. They were both making a Novena on that account, and had even gone to the expense of burning a round dozen of candles before the good St. Joseph, for his conversion. When Hector accidentally discovered the fact, he offered to pay for the candles, and was distressed at not being permitted to do so.

Suzanne had been in the city more than a month. It was already the close of February, and the air was flower-scented, moist, and deliciously mild.

"As I said: women, my dear Maman Chavan"—

"Let us hear no more about women!" cried Suzanne, impatiently. "*Cher Maître!* but Hector can be tiresome when he wants. Talk, talk; to say what in the end?"

"Quite right, my cousin; when I might have been saying how charming you are this morning. But don't think that I have n't noticed it," and he looked at her with a deliberation that quite unsettled her. She took a letter from her pocket and handed it to him.

"Here, read all the nice things mamma has to say of you, and the love messages she sends to you." He accepted the several closely written sheets from her and began to look over them.

"Ah, *la bonne tante*," he laughed, when he came to the tender passages that referred to himself. He had pushed aside the glass of wine that he had only partly filled at the beginning of breakfast and that he had scarcely touched. Maman Chavan again replenished her own. She also lighted a cigarette. So did Suzanne, who was learning to smoke. Hector did not smoke; he did not use tobacco in any form, he always said to those who offered him cigars.

Suzanne rested her elbows on the table, adjusted the ruffles about her wrists, puffed awkwardly at her cigarette that kept going out, and hummed the Kyrie Eleison that she had heard so beautifully rendered an hour before at the Cathedral, while she gazed off into the green depths of the garden. Maman Chavan slipped a little silver medal toward her, accompanying the action with a pantomime that Suzanne readily understood. She, in turn, secretly and adroitly transferred the medal to Hector's coat-pocket. He noticed the action plainly enough, but pretended not to.

"Natchitoches has n't changed," he commented. "The everlasting *can-cans!* when will they have done with them? This is n't little Athénaïse Miché, getting married! *Sapristi!* but it makes one old! And old Papa Jean-Pierre only dead now? I thought he was out of purgatory five years ago. And who is this Laballière? One of the Laballières of St. James?"

"St. James, *mon cher*. Monsieur Alphonse Laballière; an aristocrat from the 'golden coast.' But it is a history, if you will believe me. *Figurez vouz*, Maman Chavan,—*pensez donc, mon ami*"—And with much dramatic fire, during which the cigarette went irrevocably out, she proceeded to narrate her experiences with Laballière.

"Impossible!" exclaimed Hector when the climax was reached; but his indignation was not so patent as she would have liked it to be.

"And to think of an affront like that going unpunished!" was Maman Chavan's more sympathetic comment.

"Oh, the scholars were only too ready to offer violence to poor little André, but that, you can understand, I would not permit. And now, here is mamma gone completely over to him; entrapped, God only knows how!"

"Yes," agreed Hector, "I see he has been sending her tamales and *boudin blanc.*"

"*Boudin blanc*, my friend! If it were only that! But I have a stack of letters, so high,—I could show them to you,—singing of Laballière, Laballière, enough to drive one distracted. He visits her constantly. He is a man of attainment, she says, a man of courage, a man of heart; and the best of company. He has sent her a bunch of fat robins as big as a tub"—

"There is something in that—a good deal in that, mignonne," piped Maman Chavan, approvingly.

"And now *boudin blanc!* and she tells me it is the duty of a Christian to forgive. Ah, no; it's no use; mamma's ways are past finding out."

Suzanne was never in Hector's company elsewhere than at Maman Chavan's. Beside the Sunday visit, he looked in upon them sometimes at dusk, to chat for a moment or two. He often treated them to theatre tickets, and even to the opera, when business was brisk. Business meant a little note-book that he carried in his pocket, in which he sometimes dotted down orders from the country people for wine, that he sold on commission. The women always went together, unaccompanied by any male escort; trotting along, arm in arm, and brimming with enjoyment.

That same Sunday afternoon Hector walked with them a short distance when they were on their way to vespers. The three walking abreast almost occupied the narrow width of the banquette. A gentleman who had just stepped out of the Hotel Royal stood aside to better enable them to pass. He lifted his hat to Suzanne, and cast a quick glance, that pictured stupefaction and wrath, upon Hector.

"It's he!" exclaimed the girl, melodramatically seizing Maman Chavan's arm.

"Who, he?"

"Laballière!"

"No!"

"Yes!"

"A handsome fellow, all the same," nodded the little lady, approvingly. Hector thought so too. The conversation again turned upon Laballière, and so continued till they reached the side door of the cathedral, where the young man left his two companions.

In the evening Laballière called upon Suzanne. Maman Chavan closed the front door carefully after he entered the small parlor, and opened the side one that looked into the privacy of the garden. Then she lighted the lamp and retired, just as Suzanne entered.

The girl bowed a little stiffly, if it may be said that she did anything stiffly. "Monsieur Laballière." That was all she said.

"Mademoiselle St. Denys Godolph," and that was all he said. But ceremony did not sit easily upon him.

"Mademoiselle," he began, as soon as seated, "I am here as the bearer of a message from your mother. You must understand that otherwise I would not be here."

"I do understan', sir, that you an' maman have become very warm frien's during my absence," she returned, in measured, conventional tones.

"It pleases me immensely to hear that from you," he responded, warmly; "to believe that Madame St. Denys Godolph is my friend."

Suzanne coughed more affectedly than was quite nice, and patted her glossy braids. "The message, if you please, Mr. Laballière."

"To be sure," pulling himself together from the momentary abstraction into which he had fallen in contemplating her. "Well, it's just this; your mother, you must know, has been good enough to sell me a fine bit of land—a deep strip along the bayou"—

"Impossible! *Mais*, w'at sorcery did you use to obtain such a thing of my mother, Mr. Laballière? Lan' that has been in the St. Denys Godolph family since time untole!"

"No sorcery whatever, Mademoiselle, only an appeal to your mother's intelligence and common sense; and she is well supplied with both. She wishes me to say, further, that she desires your presence very urgently and your immediate return home."

"My mother is unduly impatient, surely," replied Suzanne, with chilling politeness.

"May I ask, mademoiselle," he broke in, with an abruptness that was startling, "the name of the man with whom you were walking this afternoon?"

She looked at him with unaffected astonishment, and told him: "I hardly understan' yo' question. That gentleman is Mr. Hector Santien, of one of the firs' families of Natchitoches; a warm ole frien' an' far distant relative of mine."

"Oh, that's his name, is it, Hector Santien? Well, please don't walk on the New Orleans streets again with Mr. Hector Santien."

"Yo' remarks would be insulting if they were not so highly amusing, Mr. Laballière."

"I beg your pardon if I am insulting; and I have no desire to be amusing," and then Laballière lost his head. "You are at liberty to walk the streets with whom you please, of course," he blurted, with ill-suppressed passion, "but if I encounter Mr. Hector Santien in your company again, in public, I shall wring his neck, then and there, as I would a chicken; I shall break every bone in his body"—Suzanne had arisen.

"You have said enough, sir. I even desire no explanation of yo' words."

"I did n't intend to explain them," he retorted, stung by the insinuation.

"You will escuse me further," she requested icily, motioning to retire.

"Not till—oh, not till you have forgiven me," he cried impulsively, barring her exit; for repentance had come swiftly this time.

But she did not forgive him. "I can wait," she said. Then he stepped aside and she passed by him without a second glance.

She sent word to Hector the following day to come to her. And when he was there, in the late afternoon, they walked together to the end of the vine-sheltered gallery,—where the air was redolent with the odor of spring blossoms.

"Hector," she began, after a while, "some one has told me I should not be seen upon the streets of New Orleans with you."

He was trimming a long rose-stem with his sharp penknife. He did not stop nor start, nor look embarrassed, nor anything of the sort.

"Indeed!" he said.

"But, you know," she went on, "if the saints came down from heaven to tell me there was a reason for it, I could n't believe them."

"You wouldn't believe them, *ma petite Suzanne*?" He was getting all the thorns off nicely, and stripping away the heavy lower leaves.

"I want you to look me in the face, Hector, and tell me if there is any reason."

He snapped the knife-blade and replaced the knife in his pocket; then he looked in her eyes, so unflinchingly, that she hoped and believed it presaged a confession of innocence that she would gladly have accepted. But he said indifferently: "Yes, there are reasons."

"Then I say there are not," she exclaimed excitedly; "you are amusing your-self—laughing at me, as you always do. There are no reasons that I will hear or believe. You will walk the streets with me, will you not, Hector?" she entreated, "and go to church with me on Sunday; and, and—oh, it's nonsense, nonsense for you to say things like that!"

He held the rose by its long, hardy stem, and swept it lightly and caressingly across her forehead, along her cheek, and over her pretty mouth and chin, as a lover might have done with his lips. He noticed how the red rose left a crimson stain behind it.

She had been standing, but now she sank upon the bench that was there, and buried her face in her palms. A slight convulsive movement of the muscles indicated a suppressed sob.

"Ah, Suzanne, Suzanne, you are not going to make yourself unhappy about a *bon à rien* like me. Come, look at me; tell me that you are not." He drew her hands down from her face; and held them a while, bidding her good-by. His own face wore the quizzical look it often did, as if he were laughing at her.

"That work at the store is telling on your nerves, *mignonne*. Promise me that you will go back to the country. That will be best."

"Oh, yes; I am going back home, Hector."

"That is right, little cousin," and he patted her hands kindly, and laid them both down gently into her lap.

He did not return; neither during the week nor the following Sunday. Then Suzanne told Maman Chavan she was going home. The girl was not too deeply in love with Hector: but imagination counts for something, and so does youth.

LABALLIÈRE WAS ON THE TRAIN with her. She felt, somehow, that he would be. And yet she did not dream that he had watched and waited for her each morning since he parted from her.

He went to her without preliminary of manner or speech, and held out his hand; she extended her own unhesitatingly. She could not understand why, and she was a little too weary to strive to do so. It seemed as though the sheer force of his will would carry him to the goal of his wishes.

He did not weary her with attentions during the time they were together. He sat apart from her, conversing for the most time with friends and acquaintances who belonged in the sugar district through which they traveled in the early part of the day.

She wondered why he had ever left that section to go up into Natchitoches. Then she wondered if he did not mean to speak to her at all. As if he had read the thought, he went and sat down beside her.

He showed her, away off across the country, where his mother lived, and his brother Alcée, and his cousin Clarisse.

ON SUNDAY MORNING, WHEN MAMAN Chavan strove to sound the depth of Hector's feeling for Suzanne, he told her again:

"Women, my dear Maman Chavan, you know how it is with me in regard to women," and he refilled her glass from the bottle of sauterne.

"*Farceur va!*" and Maman Chavan laughed, and her fat shoulders quivered under the white *volante* she wore.

A day or two later, Hector was walking down Canal Street at four in the afternoon. He might have posed, as he was, for a fashion-plate. He looked not to the right nor to the left; not even at the women who passed by. Some of them turned to look at him.

When he approached the corner of Royal, a young man who stood there nudged his companion.

"You know who that is?" he said, indicating Hector.

"No; who?"

"Well, you are an innocent. Why, that's Deroustan, the most notorious gambler in New Orleans."

In Sabine

The sight of a human habitation, even if it was a rude log cabin with a mud chimney at one end, was a very gratifying one to Grégoire. He had come out of Natchitoches parish, and had been riding a great part of the day through the big lonesome parish of Sabine. He was not following the regular Texas road, but, led by his erratic fancy, was pushing toward the Sabine River by circuitous paths through the rolling pine forests.

As he approached the cabin in the clearing, he discerned behind a palisade of pine saplings an old negro man chopping wood.

"Howdy, Uncle," called out the young fellow, reining his horse. The negro looked up in blank amazement at so unexpected an apparition, but he only answered: "How you do, suh," accompanying his speech by a series of polite nods.

"Who lives yere?"

"Hit's Mas' Bud Aiken w'at live' heah, suh."

"Well, if Mr. Bud Aiken c'n afford to hire a man to chop his wood, I reckon he won't grudge me a bite o' suppa an' a couple hours' res' on his gall'ry. W'at you say, ole man?"

"I say dit Mas' Bud Aiken don't hires me to chop 'ood. Ef I don't chop dis heah, his wife got it to do. Dat w'y I chops 'ood, suh. Go right 'long in, suh; you g'me fine Mas' Bud some'eres roun', ef he ain't drunk an' gone to bed."

Grégoire, glad to stretch his legs, dismounted, and led his horse into the small inclosure which surrounded the cabin. An unkempt, vicious-looking little Texas pony stopped nibbling the stubble there to look maliciously at him and his fine sleek horse, as they passed by. Back of the hut, and running plumb up against the pine wood, was a small, ragged specimen of a cotton-field.

Grégoire was rather undersized, with a square, well-knit figure, upon which his clothes sat well and easily. His corduroy trousers were thrust into the legs of his boots; he wore a blue flannel shirt; his coat was thrown across the saddle. In his keen black eyes had come a puzzled expression, and he tugged thoughtfully at the brown moustache that lightly shaded his upper lip.

He was trying to recall when and under what circumstances he had before heard the name of Bud Aiken. But Bud Aiken himself saved

Grégoire the trouble of further speculation on the subject. He appeared suddenly in the small doorway, which his big body quite filled; and then Grégoire remembered. This was the disreputable so-called "Texan" who a year ago had run away with and married Baptiste Choupic's pretty daughter, 'Tite Reine, yonder on Bayou Pierre, in Natchitoches parish. A vivid picture of the girl as he remembered her appeared to him: her trim rounded figure; her piquant face with its saucy black coquettish eyes; her little exacting, imperious ways that had obtained for her the nickname of 'Tite Reine, little queen. Grégoire had known her at the 'Cadian balls that he sometimes had the hardihood to attend.

These pleasing recollections of 'Tite Reine lent a warmth that might otherwise have been lacking to Grégoire's manner, when he greeted her husband.

"I hope I fine you well, Mr. Aiken," he exclaimed cordially, as he approached and extended his hand.

"You find me damn' porely, suh; but you 've got the better o' me, ef I may so say."

He was a big good-looking brute, with a straw-colored "horse-shoe" moustache quite concealing his mouth, and a several days' growth of stubble on his rugged face. He was fond of reiterating that women's admiration had wrecked his life, quite forgetting to mention the early and sustained influence of "Pike's Magnolia" and other brands, and wholly ignoring certain inborn propensities capable of wrecking unaided any ordinary existence. He had been lying down, and looked frouzy and half asleep.

"Ef I may so say, you've got the better o' me, Mr.—er"—

"Santien, Grégoire Santien. I have the pleasure o' knowin' the lady you married, suh; an' I think I met you befo',—some-w'ere o' 'nother," Grégoire added vaguely.

"Oh," drawled Aiken, waking up, "one o' them Red River Sanchuns!" and his face brightened at the prospect before him of enjoying the society of one of the Santien boys. "Mortimer!" he called in ringing chest tones worthy a commander at the head of his troop. The negro had rested his axe and appeared to be listening to their talk, though he was too far to hear what they said.

"Mortimer, come along here an' take my frien' Mr. Sanchun's hoss. Git a move thar, git a move!" Then turning toward the entrance of the cabin he called back through the open door: "Rain!" it was his way of pronouncing 'Tite Reine's name. "Rain!" he cried again peremptorily;

and turning to Grégoire: "she's 'tendin' to some or other housekeepin' truck." 'Tite Reine was back in the yard feeding the solitary pig which they owned, and which Aiken had mysteriously driven up a few days before, saying he had bought it at Many.

Grégoire could hear her calling out as she approached: "I'm comin', Bud. Yere I come. W'at you want, Bud?" breathlessly, as she appeared in the door frame and looked out upon the narrow sloping gallery where stood the two men. She seemed to Grégoire to have changed a good deal. She was thinner, and her eyes were larger, with an alert, uneasy look in them; he fancied the startled expression came from seeing him there unexpectedly. She wore cleanly homespun garments, the same she had brought with her from Bayou Pierre; but her shoes were in shreds. She uttered only a low, smothered exclamation when she saw Grégoire.

"Well, is that all you got to say to my frien' Mr. Sanchun? That's the way with them Cajuns," Aiken offered apologetically to his guest; "ain't got sense enough to know a white man when they see one." Grégoire took her hand.

"I'm mighty glad to see you, 'Tite Heine," he said from his heart. She had for some reason been unable to speak; now she panted somewhat hysterically:—

"You mus' escuse me, Mista Grégoire. It's the truth I did n' know you firs', stan'in' up there." A deep flush had supplanted the former pallor of her face, and her eyes shone with tears and ill-concealed excitement.

"I thought you all lived yonda in Grant," remarked Grégoire carelessly, making talk for the purpose of diverting Aiken's attention away from his wife's evident embarrassment, which he himself was at a loss to understand.

"Why, we did live a right smart while in Grant; but Grant ain't no parish to make a livin' in. Then I tried Winn and Caddo a spell; they was n't no better. But I tell you, suh, Sabine's a damn' sight worse than any of 'em. Why, a man can't git a drink o' whiskey here without going out of the parish fer it, or across into Texas. I'm fixin' to sell out an' try Vernon."

Bud Aiken's household belongings surely would not count for much in the contemplated "selling out." The one room that constituted his home was extremely bare of furnishing,—a cheap bed, a pine table, and a few chairs, that was all. On a rough shelf were some paper parcels representing the larder. The mud daubing had fallen out here and there from between the logs of the cabin; and into the largest of these apertures had been thrust pieces of ragged bagging and wisps of cotton. A tin basin outside on the gallery offered the only bathing facilities to be seen. Notwithstanding these drawbacks, Grégoire announced his intention of passing the night with Aiken.

"I'm jus' goin' to ask the privilege o' layin' down yere on yo' gall'ry to-night, Mr. Aiken. My hoss ain't in firs'-class trim; an' a night's res' ain't goin' to hurt him o' me either." He had begun by declaring his intention of pushing on across the Sabine, but an imploring look from 'Tite Reine's eyes had stayed the words upon his lips. Never had he seen in a woman's eyes a look of such heartbroken entreaty. He resolved on the instant to know the meaning of it before setting foot on Texas soil. Grégoire had never learned to steel his heart against a woman's eyes, no matter what language they spoke.

An old patchwork quilt folded double and a moss pillow which 'Tite Reine gave him out on the gallery made a bed that was, after all, not too uncomfortable for a young fellow of rugged habits.

Grégoire slept quite soundly after he laid down upon his improvised bed at nine o'clock. He was awakened toward the middle of the night by some one gently shaking him. It was 'Tite Reine stooping over him; he could see her plainly, for the moon was shining. She had not removed the clothing she had worn during the day; but her feet were bare and looked wonderfully small and white. He arose on his elbow, wide awake at once. "W'y, 'Tite Reine! w'at the devil you mean? w'ere's yo' husban'?"

"The house kin fall on 'im, 'ten goin' wake up Bud w'en he's sleepin'; he drink' too much." Now that she had aroused Grégoire, she stood up, and sinking her face in her bended arm like a child, began to cry softly. In an instant he was on his feet.

"My God, 'Tite Reine! w'at's the matta? you got to tell me w'at's the matta." He could no longer recognize the imperious 'Tite Reine, whose will had been the law in her father's household. He led her to the edge of the low gallery and there they sat down.

Grégoire loved women. He liked their nearness, their atmosphere; the tones of their voices and the things they said; their ways of moving and turning about; the brushing of their garments when they passed him by pleased him. He was fleeing now from the pain that a woman had inflicted upon him. When any overpowering sorrow came to Grégoire he felt a singular longing to cross the Sabine River and lose himself in Texas. He had done this once before when his home, the old Santien place, had gone into the hands of creditors. The sight of 'Tite Reine's distress now moved him painfully.

"W'at is it, 'Tite Reine? tell me w'at it is," he kept asking her. She was attempting to dry her eyes on her coarse sleeve. He drew a handkerchief from his back pocket and dried them for her.

"They all well, yonda?" she asked, haltingly, "my popa? my moma? the chil'en?" Grégoire knew no more of the Baptiste Choupic family than the post beside him. Nevertheless he answered: "They all right well, 'Tite Reine, but they mighty lonesome of you."

"My popa, he got a putty good crop this yea'?"

"He made right smart o' cotton fo' Bayou Pierre."

"He done haul it to the relroad?"

"No, he ain't quite finish pickin'."

"I hope they all ent sole 'Putty Girl'?" she inquired solicitously.

"Well, I should say not! Yo' pa says they ain't anotha piece o' hossflesh in the pa'ish he'd want to swap fo' 'Putty Girl.'" She turned to him with vague but fleeting amazement,—"Putty Girl" was a cow!

The autumn night was heavy about them. The black forest seemed to have drawn nearer; its shadowy depths were filled with the gruesome noises that inhabit a southern forest at night time.

"Ain't you 'fraid sometimes yere, 'Tite Reine?" Grégoire asked, as he felt a light shiver run through him at the weirdness of the scene.

"No," she answered promptly, "I ent 'fred o' nothin' 'cep' Bud."

"Then he treats you mean? I thought so!"

"Mista Grégoire," drawing close to him and whispering in his face, "Bud's killin' me." He clasped her arm, holding her near him, while an expression of profound pity escaped him. "Nobody don' know, 'cep' Unc' Mort'mer," she went on. "I tell you, he beats me; my back an' arms— you ought to see—it's all blue. He would 'a' choke' me to death one day w'en he was drunk, if Unc' Mort'mer had n' make 'im lef go—with his axe ov' his head." Grégoire glanced back over his shoulder toward the room where the man lay sleeping. He was wondering if it would really be a criminal act to go then and there and shoot the top of Bud Aiken's head off. He himself would hardly have considered it a crime, but he was not sure of how others might regard the act.

"That's w'y I wake you up, to tell you," she continued. "Then sometime' he plague me mos' crazy; he tell me't ent no preacher, it's a Texas drummer w'at marry him an' me; an' w'en I don' know w'at way to turn no mo', he say no, it's a Meth'dis' archbishop, an' keep on laughin' 'bout me, an' I don' know w'at the truth!"

Then again, she told how Bud had induced her to mount the vicious little mustang "Buckeye," knowing that the little brute would n't carry a woman; and how it had amused him to witness her distress and terror when she was thrown to the ground.

"If I would know how to read an' write, an' had some pencil an' paper, it's long 'go I would wrote to my popa. But it's no pos'-office, it's no relroad,—nothin' in Sabine. An' you know, Mista Grégoire, Bud say he's goin' carry me yonda to Vernon, an' fu'ther off yet,—'way yonda, an' he's goin' turn me loose. Oh, don' leave me yere, Mista Grégoire! don' leave me behine you!" she entreated, breaking once more into sobs.

"'Tite Reine," he answered, "do you think I'm such a low-down scound'el as to leave you yere with that"—He finished the sentence mentally, not wishing to offend the ears of 'Tite Reine.

They talked on a good while after that. She would not return to the room where her husband lay; the nearness of a friend had already emboldened her to inward revolt. Grégoire induced her to lie down and rest upon the quilt that she had given to him for a bed. She did so, and broken down by fatigue was soon fast asleep.

He stayed seated on the edge of the gallery and began to smoke cigarettes which he rolled himself of perique tobacco. He might have gone in and shared Bud Aiken's bed, but preferred to stay there near 'Tite Reine. He watched the two horses, tramping slowly about the lot, cropping the dewy wet tufts of grass.

Grégoire smoked on. He only stopped when the moon sank down behind the pine-trees, and the long deep shadow reached out and enveloped him. Then he could no longer see and follow the filmy smoke from his cigarette, and he threw it away. Sleep was pressing heavily upon him. He stretched himself full length upon the rough bare boards of the gallery and slept until day-break.

Bud Aiken's satisfaction was very genuine when he learned that Grégoire proposed spending the day and another night with him. He had already recognized in the young creole a spirit not altogether uncongenial to his own.

'Tite Reine cooked breakfast for them. She made coffee; of course there was no milk to add to it, but there was sugar. From a meal bag that stood in the corner of the room she took a measure of meal, and with it made a pone of corn bread. She fried slices of salt pork. Then Bud sent her into the field to pick cotton with old Uncle Mortimer. The negro's cabin was the counterpart of their own, but stood quite a distance away hidden in the woods. He and Aiken worked the crop on shares.

Early in the day Bud produced a grimy pack of cards from behind a parcel of sugar on the shelf. Grégoire threw the cards into the fire and replaced them with a spic and span new "deck" that he took from his saddle-bags. He also brought forth from the same receptacle a bottle of whiskey, which he presented to his host, saying that he himself had no further use for it, as he had "sworn off" since day before yesterday, when he had made a fool of himself in Cloutierville.

They sat at the pine table smoking and playing cards all the morning, only desisting when 'Tite Reine came to serve them with the gumbo-filé that she had come out of the field to cook at noon. She could afford to treat a guest to chicken gumbo, for she owned a half dozen chickens that Uncle Mortimer had presented to her at various times. There were only two spoons, and 'Tite Reine had to wait till the men had finished before eating her soup. She waited for Grégoire's spoon, though her husband was the first to get through. It was a very childish whim.

In the afternoon she picked cotton again; and the men played cards, smoked, and Bud drank.

It was a very long time since Bud Aiken had enjoyed himself so well, and since he had encountered so sympathetic and appreciative a listener to the story of his eventful career. The story of 'Tite Reine's fall from the horse he told with much spirit, mimicking quite skillfully the way in which she had complained of never being permitted "to teck a li'le pleasure," whereupon he had kindly suggested horseback riding. Grégoire enjoyed the story amazingly, which encouraged Aiken to relate many more of a similar character. As the afternoon wore on, all formality of address between the two had disappeared: they were "Bud" and "Grégoire" to each other, and Grégoire had delighted Aiken's soul by promising to spend a week with him. 'Tite Reine was also touched by the spirit of recklessness in the air; it moved her to fry two chickens for supper. She fried them deliciously in bacon fat. After supper she again arranged Grégoire's bed out on the gallery.

The night fell calm and beautiful, with the delicious odor of the pines floating upon the air. But the three did not sit up to enjoy it. Before the stroke of nine, Aiken had already fallen upon his bed unconscious of everything about him in the heavy drunken sleep that would hold him fast through the night. It even clutched him more relentlessly than usual, thanks to Grégoire's free gift of whiskey.

The sun was high when he awoke. He lifted his voice and called imperiously for 'Tite Reine, wondering that the coffee-pot was not on the hearth, and marveling still more that he did not hear her voice in quick response with its, "I'm comin', Bud. Yere I come." He called again and again. Then he arose and looked out through the back door to see if she were picking cotton in the field, but she was not there. He dragged himself to the front entrance. Grégoire's bed was still on the gallery, but the young fellow was nowhere to be seen.

Uncle Mortimer had come into the yard, not to cut wood this time, but to pick up the axe which was his own property, and lift it to his shoulder.

"Mortimer," called out Aiken, "whur's my wife?" at the same time advancing toward the negro. Mortimer stood still, waiting for him. "Whur's my wife an' that Frenchman? Speak out, I say, before I send you to h—l."

Uncle Mortimer never had feared Bud Aiken; and with the trusty axe upon his shoulder, he felt a double hardihood in the man's presence. The old fellow passed the back of his black, knotty hand unctuously over his lips, as though he relished in advance the words that were about to pass them. He spoke carefully and deliberately:

"Miss Reine," he said, "I reckon she mus' of done struck Natchitoches pa'ish sometime to'ard de middle o' de night, on dat 'ar swif' hoss o' Mr. Sanchun's."

Aiken uttered a terrific oath. "Saddle up Buckeye," he yelled, "before I count twenty, or I'll rip the black hide off yer. Quick, thar! Thur ain't nothin' four-footed top o' this earth that Buckeye can't run down." Uncle Mortimer scratched his head dubiously, as he answered:—

"Yas, Mas' Bud, but you see, Mr. Sanchun, he done cross de Sabine befo' sun-up on Buckeye."

A Very Fine Fiddle

When the half dozen little ones were hungry, old Cléophas would take the fiddle from its flannel bag and play a tune upon it. Perhaps it was to drown their cries, or their hunger, or his conscience, or all three. One day Fifine, in a rage, stamped her small foot and clinched her little hands, and declared:

"It's no two way'! I'm goin' smash it, dat fiddle, some day in a t'ousan' piece'!"

"You mus' n' do dat, Fifine," expostulated her father. "Dat fiddle been ol'er 'an you an' me t'ree time' put togedder. You done yaird me tell often 'nough 'bout dat *Italien* w'at give it to me w'en he die, 'long yonder befo' de war. An' he say, 'Cléophas, dat fiddle—dat one part my life—w'at goin' live w'en I be dead—*Dieu merci!*' You talkin' too fas', Fifine."

"Well, I'm goin' do some'in' wid dat fiddle, *va!*" returned the daughter, only half mollified. "Mine w'at I say."

So once when there were great carryings-on up at the big plantation—no end of ladies and gentlemen from the city, riding, driving, dancing, and making music upon all manner of instruments—Fifine, with the fiddle in its flannel bag, stole away and up to the big house where these festivities were in progress.

No one noticed at first the little barefoot girl seated upon a step of the veranda and watching, lynx-eyed, for her opportunity.

"It's one fiddle I got for sell," she announced, resolutely, to the first who questioned her.

It was very funny to have a shabby little girl sitting there wanting to sell a fiddle, and the child was soon surrounded.

The lustreless instrument was brought forth and examined, first with amusement, but soon very seriously, especially by three gentlemen: one with very long hair that hung down, another with equally long hair that stood up, the third with no hair worth mentioning.

These three turned the fiddle upside down and almost inside out. They thumped upon it, and listened. They scraped upon it, and listened. They walked into the house with it, and out of the house with it, and into remote corners with it. All this with much putting of heads together, and talking together in familiar and unfamiliar languages. And, finally, they sent Fifine away with a fiddle twice as beautiful as the one she had brought, and a roll of money besides!

The child was dumb with astonishment, and away she flew. But when she stopped beneath a big chinaberry-tree, to further scan the roll of money, her wonder was redoubled. There was far more than she could count, more than she had ever dreamed of possessing. Certainly enough to top the old cabin with new shingles; to put shoes on all the little bare feet and food into the hungry mouths. Maybe enough—and Fifine's heart fairly jumped into her throat at the vision—maybe enough to buy Blanchette and her tiny calf that Unc' Siméon wanted to sell!

"It's jis like you say, Fifine," murmured old Cléophas, huskily, when he had played upon the new fiddle that night. "It's one fine fiddle; an' like you say, it shine' like satin. But some way or udder, 't ain' de same. Yair, Fifine, take it—put it 'side. I b'lieve, me, I ain' goin' play de fiddle no mo'."

Beyond the Bayou

The bayou curved like a crescent around the point of land on which La Folle's cabin stood. Between the stream and the hut lay a big abandoned field, where cattle were pastured when the bayou supplied them with water enough. Through the woods that spread back into unknown regions the woman had drawn an imaginary line, and past this circle she never stepped. This was the form of her only mania.

She was now a large, gaunt black woman, past thirty-five. Her real name was Jacqueline, but every one on the plantation called her La Folle, because in childhood she had been frightened literally "out of her senses," and had never wholly regained them.

It was when there had been skirmishing and sharpshooting all day in the woods. Evening was near when P'tit Maître, black with powder and crimson with blood, had staggered into the cabin of Jacqueline's mother, his pursuers close at his heels. The sight had stunned her childish reason.

She dwelt alone in her solitary cabin, for the rest of the quarters had long since been removed beyond her sight and knowledge. She had more physical strength than most men, and made her patch of cotton and corn and tobacco like the best of them. But of the world beyond the bayou she had long known nothing, save what her morbid fancy conceived.

People at Bellissime had grown used to her and her way, and they thought nothing of it. Even when "Old Mis'" died, they did not wonder that La Folle had not crossed the bayou, but had stood upon her side of it, wailing and lamenting.

P'tit Maître was now the owner of Bellissime. He was a middle-aged man, with a family of beautiful daughters about him, and a little son whom La Folle loved as if he had been her own. She called him Chéri, and so did every one else because she did.

None of the girls had ever been to her what Chéri was. They had each and all loved to be with her, and to listen to her wondrous stories of things that always happened "yonda, beyon' de bayou."

But none of them had stroked her black hand quite as Chéri did, nor rested their heads against her knee so confidingly, nor fallen asleep in her arms as he used to do. For Chéri hardly did such things now, since he had become the proud possessor of a gun, and had had his black curls cut off.

That summer—the summer Chéri gave La Folle two black curls tied with a knot of red ribbon—the water ran so low in the bayou that even the little children at Bellissime were able to cross it on foot, and the cattle were sent to pasture down by the river. La Folle was sorry when they were gone, for she loved these dumb companions well, and liked to feel that they were there, and to hear them browsing by night up to her own inclosure.

It was Saturday afternoon, when the fields were deserted. The men had flocked to a neighboring village to do their week's trading, and the women were occupied with household affairs,—La Folle as well as the others. It was then she mended and washed her handful of clothes, scoured her house, and did her baking.

In this last employment she never forgot Chéri. To-day she had fashioned croquignoles of the most fantastic and alluring shapes for him. So when she saw the boy come trudging across the old field with his gleaming little new rifle on his shoulder, she called out gayly to him, "Chéri! Chéri!"

But Chéri did not need the summons, for he was coming straight to her. His pockets all bulged out with almonds and raisins and an orange that he had secured for her from the very fine dinner which had been given that day up at his father's house.

He was a sunny-faced youngster of ten. When he had emptied his pockets, La Folle patted his round red cheek, wiped his soiled hands on her apron, and smoothed his hair. Then she watched him as, with his cakes in his hand, he crossed her strip of cotton back of the cabin, and disappeared into the wood.

He had boasted of the things he was going to do with his gun out there.

"You think they got plenty deer in the wood, La Folle?" he had inquired, with the calculating air of an experienced hunter.

"*Non, non,!*" the woman laughed. "Don't you look fo' no deer, Chéri. Dat's too big. But you bring La Folle one good fat squirrel fo' her dinner to-morrow, an' she goin' be satisfi'."

"One squirrel ain't a bite. I'll bring you mo' 'an one, La Folle," he had boasted pompously as he went away.

When the woman, an hour later, heard the report of the boy's rifle close to the wood's edge, she would have thought nothing of it if a sharp cry of distress had not followed the sound.

She withdrew her arms from the tub of suds in which they had been plunged, dried them upon her apron, and as quickly as her trembling limbs would bear her, hurried to the spot whence the ominous report had come.

It was as she feared. There she found Chéri stretched upon the ground, with his rifle beside him. He moaned piteously:—

"I'm dead, La Folle! I'm dead! I'm gone!"

"*Non, non!*" she exclaimed resolutely, as she knelt beside him. "Put you' arm 'roun' La Folle's nake, Chéri. Dat's nuttin'; dat goin' be nuttin'." She lifted him in her powerful arms.

Chéri had carried his gun muzzle-downward. He had stumbled,—he did not know how. He only knew that he had a ball lodged somewhere in his leg, and he thought that his end was at hand. Now, with his head upon the woman's shoulder, he moaned and wept with pain and fright.

"Oh, La Folle! La Folle! it hurt so bad! I can' stan' it, La Folle!"

"Don't cry, mon bébé mon bébé, mon Chéri!" the woman spoke soothingly as she covered the ground with long strides. "La Folle goin' mine you; Doctor Bonfils goin' come make *mon Chéri* well agin."

She had reached the abandoned field. As she crossed it with her precious burden, she looked constantly and restlessly from side to side. A terrible fear was upon her,—the fear of the world beyond the bayou, the morbid and insane dread she had been under since childhood.

When she was at the bayou's edge she stood there, and shouted for help as if a life depended upon it:—

"Oh, P'tit Maître! P'tit Maître! Venez done! Au secours! Au secours!"

No voice responded. Chéri's hot tears were scalding her neck. She called for each and every one upon the place, and still no answer came.

She shouted, she wailed; but whether her voice remained unheard or unheeded, no reply came to her frenzied cries. And all the while Chéri moaned and wept and entreated to be taken home to his mother.

La Folle gave a last despairing look around her. Extreme terror was upon her. She clasped the child close against her breast, where he could feel her heart beat like a muffled hammer. Then shutting her eyes, she ran suddenly down the shallow bank of the bayou, and never stopped till she had climbed the opposite shore.

She stood there quivering an instant as she opened her eyes. Then she plunged into the footpath through the trees.

She spoke no more to Chéri, but muttered constantly, "Bon Dieu, ayez pitié La Folle! Bon Dieu, ayez pitié moi!"

Instinct seemed to guide her. When the pathway spread clear and smooth enough before her, she again closed her eyes tightly against the sight of that unknown and terrifying world.

A child, playing in some weeds, caught sight of her as she neared the quarters. The little one uttered a cry of dismay.

"La Folle!" she screamed, in her piercing treble. "La Folle done cross de bayer!"

Quickly the cry passed down the line of cabins.

"Yonda, La Folle done cross de bayou!"

Children, old men, old women, young ones with infants in their arms, flocked to doors and windows to see this awe-inspiring spectacle. Most of them shuddered with superstitious dread of what it might portend.

"She totin' Chéri!" some of them shouted.

Some of the more daring gathered about her, and followed at her heels, only to fall back with new terror when she turned her distorted face upon them. Her eyes were bloodshot and the saliva had gathered in a white foam on her black lips.

Some one had run ahead of her to where P'tit Maître sat with his family and guests upon the gallery.

"P'tit Maître! La Folle done cross de bayou! Look her! Look her yonda totin' Chéri!" This startling intimation was the first which they had of the woman's approach.

She was now near at hand. She walked with long strides. Her eyes were fixed desperately before her, and she breathed heavily, as a tired ox.

At the foot of the stairway, which she could not have mounted, she laid the boy in his father's arms. Then the world that had looked red to La Folle suddenly turned black,—like that day she had seen powder and blood.—

She reeled for an instant. Before a sustaining arm could reach her, she fell heavily to the ground.

When La Folle regained consciousness, she was at home again, in her own cabin and upon her own bed. The moon rays, streaming in through the open door and windows, gave what light was needed to the old black mammy who stood at the table concocting a tisane of fragrant herbs. It was very late.

Others who had come, and found that the stupor clung to her, had gone again. P'tit Maître had been there, and with him Doctor Bonfils, who said that La Folle might die.

But death had passed her by. The voice was very clear and steady with which she spoke to Tante Lizette, brewing her tisane there in a corner.

"Ef you will give me one good drink tisane, Tante Lizette, I b'lieve I'm goin' sleep, me."

And she did sleep; so soundly, so healthfully, that old Lizette without compunction stole softly away, to creep back through the moonlit fields to her own cabin in the new quarters.

The first touch of the cool gray morning awoke La Folle. She arose, calmly, as if no tempest had shaken and threatened her existence but yesterday.

She donned her new blue cottonade and white apron, for she remembered that this was Sunday. When she had made for herself a cup of strong black coffee, and drunk it with relish, she quitted the cabin and walked across the old familiar field to the bayou's edge again.

She did not stop there as she had always done before, but crossed with a long, steady stride as if she had done this all her life.

When she had made her way through the brush and scrub cottonwood-trees that lined the opposite bank, she found herself upon the border of a field where the white, bursting cotton, with the dew upon it, gleamed for acres and acres like frosted silver in the early dawn.

La Folle drew a long, deep breath as she gazed across the country. She walked slowly and uncertainly, like one who hardly knows how, looking about her as she went.

The cabins, that yesterday had sent a clamor of voices to pursue her, were quiet now. No one was yet astir at Bellissime. Only the birds that darted here and there from hedges were awake, and singing their matins.

When La Folle came to the broad stretch of velvety lawn that surrounded the house, she moved slowly and with delight over the springy turf, that was delicious beneath her tread.

She stopped to find whence came those perfumes that were assailing her senses with memories from a time far gone.

There they were, stealing up to her from the thousand blue violets that peeped out from green, luxuriant beds. There they were, showering down from the big waxen bells of the magnolias far above her head, and from the jessamine clumps around her.

There were roses, too, without number. To right and left palms spread in broad and graceful curves. It all looked like enchantment beneath the sparkling sheen of dew.

When La Folle had slowly and cautiously mounted the many steps that led up to the veranda, she turned to look back at the perilous ascent she had made. Then she caught sight of the river, bending like a silver bow at the foot of Bellissime. Exultation possessed her soul.

La Folle rapped softly upon a door near at hand. Chéri's mother soon cautiously opened it. Quickly and cleverly she dissembled the astonishment she felt at seeing La Folle.

"Ah, La Folle! Is it you, so early?"

"*Oui*, madame. I come ax how my po' li'le Chéri to, 's mo'nin'."

"He is feeling easier, thank you, La Folle. Dr. Bonfils says it will be nothing serious. He's sleeping now. Will you come back when he awakes?"

"*Non*, madame. I'm goin' wait yair tell Chéri wake up." La Folle seated herself upon the topmost step of the veranda.

A look of wonder and deep content crept into her face as she watched for the first time the sun rise upon the new, the beautiful world beyond the bayou.

Old Aunt Peggy

When the war was over, old Aunt Peggy went to Monsieur, and said:—

"Massa, I ain't never gwine to quit yer. I'm gittin' ole an' feeble, an' my days is few in dis heah lan' o' sorrow an' sin. All I axes is a li'le co'ner whar I kin set down an' wait peaceful fu de en'."

Monsieur and Madame were very much touched at this mark of affection and fidelity from Aunt Peggy. So, in the general reconstruction of the plantation which immediately followed the surrender, a nice cabin, pleasantly appointed, was set apart for the old woman. Madame did not even forget the very comfortable rocking-chair in which Aunt Peggy might "set down," as she herself feelingly expressed it, "an' wait fu de en'."

She has been rocking ever since.

At intervals of about two years Aunt Peggy hobbles up to the house, and delivers the stereotyped address which has become more than familiar:—

"Mist'ess, I's come to take a las' look at you all. Le' me look at you good. Le' me look at de chillun,—de big chillun an' de li'le chillun. Le' me look at de picters an' de photygraphts an' de pianny, an' eve'ything 'fo' it's too late. One eye is done gone, an' de udder's a-gwine fas'. Any mo'nin' yo' po' ole Aunt Peggy gwine wake up an' fin' herse'f stone-bline."

After such a visit Aunt Peggy invariably returns to her cabin with a generously filled apron.

The scruple which Monsieur one time felt in supporting a woman for so many years in idleness has entirely disappeared. Of late his attitude towards Aunt Peggy is simply one of profound astonishment,—wonder at the surprising age which an old black woman may attain when she sets her mind to it, for Aunt Peggy is a hundred and twenty-five, so she says.

It may not be true, however. Possibly she is older.

The Return of Alcibiade

M r. Fred Bartner was sorely perplexed and annoyed to find that a wheel and tire of his buggy threatened to part company.

"Ef you want," said the negro boy who drove him, "we kin stop yonda at ole M'sié Jean Ba's an' fix it; he got de bes' black-smif shop in de pa'ish on his place."

"Who in the world is old Monsieur Jean Ba," the young man inquired.

"How come, suh, you don' know old M'sié Jean Baptiste Plochel? He ole, ole. He sorter quare in he head ev' sence his son M'sié Alcibiade got kill' in de wah. Yonda he live'; whar you sees dat che'okee hedge takin' up half de road."

Little more than twelve years ago, before the "Texas and Pacific" had joined the cities of New Orleans and Shreveport with its steel bands, it was a common thing to travel through miles of central Louisiana in a buggy. Fred Bartner, a young commission merchant of New Orleans, on business bent, had made the trip in this way by easy stages from his home to a point on Cane River, within a half day's journey of Natchitoches. From the mouth of Cane River he had passed one plantation after another,—large ones and small ones. There was nowhere sight of anything like a town, except the little hamlet of Cloutierville, through which they had sped in the gray dawn. "Dat town, hit's ole, ole; mos' a hund'ed year' ole, dey say. Uh, uh, look to me like it heap ol'r an' dat," the darkey had commented. Now they were within sight of Monsieur Jean Ba's towering Cherokee hedge.

It was Christmas morning, but the sun was warm and the air so soft and mild that Bartner found the most comfortable way to wear his light overcoat was across his knees. At the entrance to the plantation he dismounted and the negro drove away toward the smithy which stood on the edge of the field.

From the end of the long avenue of magnolias that led to it, the house which confronted Bartner looked grotesquely long in comparison with its height. It was one story, of pale, yellow stucco; its massive wooden shutters were a faded green. A wide gallery, topped by the overhanging roof, encircled it.

At the head of the stairs a very old man stood. His figure was small and shrunken, his hair long and snow-white. He wore a broad, soft felt hat, and a brown plaid shawl across his bent shoulders. A tall, graceful girl stood beside him; she was clad in a warm-colored blue stuff gown. She seemed to be expostulating with the old gentleman, who evidently wanted to descend the stairs to meet the approaching visitor. Before Bartner had had time to do more than lift his hat, Monsieur Jean Ba had thrown his trembling arms about the young man and was exclaiming in his quavering old tones: "À la fin! mon fils! à la fin!" Tears started to the girl's eyes and she was rosy with confusion. "Oh, escuse him, sir; please escuse him," she whisperingly entreated, gently striving to disengage the old gentleman's arms from around the astonished Bartner. But a new line of thought seemed fortunately to take possession of Monsieur Jean Ba, for he moved away and went quickly, pattering like a baby, down the gallery. His fleecy white hair streamed out on the soft breeze, and his brown shawl flapped as he turned the corner.

Bartner, left alone with the girl, proceeded to introduce himself and to explain his presence there.

"Oh! Mr. Fred Bartna of New Orleans? The commission merchant!" she exclaimed, cordially extending her hand. "So well known in Natchitoches parish. Not *our* merchant, Mr. Bartna," she added, naively, "but jus' as welcome, all the same, at my gran'father's."

Bartner felt like kissing her, but he only bowed and seated himself in the big chair which she offered him. He wondered what was the longest time it could take to mend a buggy tire.

She sat before him with her hands pressed down into her lap, and with an eagerness and pretty air of being confidential that were extremely engaging, explained the reasons for her grandfather's singular behavior.

Years ago, her uncle Alcibiade, in going away to the war, with the cheerful assurance of youth, had promised his father that he would return to eat Christmas dinner with him. He never returned. And now, of late years, since Monsieur Jean Ba had begun to fail in body and mind, that old, unspoken hope of long ago had come back to live anew in his heart. Every Christmas Day he watched for the coming of Alcibiade.

"Ah! if you knew, Mr. Bartna, how I have endeavor' to distrac' his mine from that thought! Weeks ago, I tole to all the negroes, big and li'le, 'If one of you dare to say the word, Christmas gif', in the hearing of Monsieur Jean Baptiste, you will have to answer it to me.'"

Bartner could not recall when he had been so deeply interested in a narration.

"So las' night, Mr. Bartna, I said to grandpère, 'Pépère, you know to-morrow will be the great feas' of la Trinité; we will read our litany together in the morning and say a *chapelet*.' He did not answer a word; *il est malin, oui*. But this morning at day-light he was rapping his cane on the back gallery, calling together the negroes. Did they not know it was Christmas Day, an' a great dinner mus' be prepare' for his son Alcibiade, whom he was especting!"

"And so he has mistaken me for his son Alcibiade. It is very unfortunate," said Bartner, sympathetically. He was a good-looking, honest-faced young fellow.

The girl arose, quivering with an inspiration. She approached Bartner, and in her eagerness laid her hand upon his arm.

"Oh, Mr. Bartna, if you will do me a favor! The greates' favor of my life!"

He expressed his absolute readiness.

"Let him believe, jus' for this one Christmas day, that you are his son. Let him have that Christmas dinner with Alcibiade, that he has been longing for so many year'."

Bartner's was not a puritanical conscience, but truthfulness was a habit as well as a principle with him, and he winced. "It seems to me it would be cruel to deceive him; it would not be"—he did not like to say "right," but she guessed that he meant it.

"Oh, for that," she laughed, "you may stay as w'ite as snow, Mr. Bartna. *I* will take all the sin on my conscience. I assume all the responsibility on my shoulder'."

"Esmée!" the old man was calling as he came trotting back, "Esmée, my child," in his quavering French, "I have ordered the dinner. Go see to the arrangements of the table, and have everything faultless."

The dining-room was at the end of the house, with windows opening upon the side and back galleries. There was a high, simply carved wooden mantelpiece, bearing a wide, slanting, old-fashioned mirror that reflected the table and its occupants. The table was laden with an overabundance. Monsieur Jean Ba sat at one end, Esmée at the other, and Bartner at the side.

Two "*grif*" boys, a big black woman and a little mulatto girl waited upon them; there was a reserve force outside within easy call, and the little black and yellow faces kept bobbing up constantly above the window-sills. Windows and doors were open, and a fire of hickory branches blazed on the hearth.

Monsieur Jean Ba ate little, but that little greedily and rapidly; then he stayed in rapt contemplation of his guest.

"You will notice, Alcibiade, the flavor of the turkey," he said. "It is dressed with pecans; those big ones from the tree down on the bayou. I had them gathered expressly." The delicate and rich flavor of the nut was indeed very perceptible.

Bartner had a stupid impression of acting on the stage, and had to pull himself together every now and then to throw off the stiffness of the amateur actor. But this discomposure amounted almost to paralysis when he found Mademoiselle Esmée taking the situation as seriously as her grandfather.

"*Mon Dieu!* uncle Alcibiade, you are not eating! *Mais* w'ere have you lef' your appetite? Corbeau, fill your young master's glass. Doralise, you are neglecting Monsieur Alcibiade; he is without bread."

Monsieur Jean Ba's feeble intelligence reached out very dimly; it was like a dream which clothes the grotesque and unnatural with the semblance of reality. He shook his head up and down with pleased approbation of Esmée's "Uncle Alcibiade," that tripped so glibly on her lips. When she arranged his after-dinner *brûlot*,—a lump of sugar in a flaming teaspoonful of brandy, dropped into a tiny cup of black coffee,— he reminded her, "Your Uncle Alcibiade takes two lumps, Esmée. The scamp! he is fond of sweets. Two or three lumps, Esmée." Bartner would have relished his brûlot greatly, prepared so gracefully as it was by Esmée's deft hands, had it not been for that superfluous lump.

After dinner the girl arranged her grandfather comfortably in his big armchair on the gallery, where he loved to sit when the weather permitted. She fastened his shawl about him and laid a second one across his knees. She shook up the pillow for his head, patted his sunken cheek and kissed his forehead under the soft-brimmed hat. She left him there with the sun warming his feet and old shrunken knees.

Esmée and Bartner walked together under the magnolias. In walking they trod upon the violet borders that grew rank and sprawling, and the subtle perfume of the crushed flowers scented the air deliciously. They stooped and plucked handfuls of them. They gathered roses, too, that were blooming yet against the warm south end of the house; and they chattered and laughed like children. When they sat in the sunlight upon the low steps to arrange the flowers they had broken, Bartner's conscience began to prick him anew.

"You know," he said, "I can't stay here always, as well as I should like to. I shall have to leave presently; then your grandfather will discover that we have been deceiving him,—and you can see how cruel that will be."

"Mr. Bartna," answered Esmée, daintily holding a rosebud up to her pretty nose, "W'en I awoke this morning an' said my prayers, I prayed to the good God that He would give one happy Christmas day to my gran'father. He has answered my prayer; an' He does not sen' his gif's incomplete. He will provide.

"Mr. Bartna, this morning I agreed to take all responsibility on my shoulder', you remember? Now, I place all that responsibility on the shoulder' of the blessed Virgin."

Bartner was distracted with admiration; whether for this beautiful and consoling faith, or its charming votary, was not quite clear to him.

Every now and then Monsieur Jean Ba would call out, "Alcibiade, *mon fils!*" and Bartner would hasten to his side. Sometimes the old man had forgotten what he wanted to say. Once it was to ask if the salad had been to his liking, or if he would, perhaps, not have preferred the turkey *aux truffes*.

"Alcibiade, *mon fils!*" Again Bartner amiably answered the summons. Monsieur Jean Ba took the young man's hand affectionately in his, but limply, as children hold hands. Bartner's closed firmly around it. "Alcibiade, I am going to take a little nap now. If Robert McFarlane comes while I am sleeping, with more talk of wanting to buy Nég Sévérin, tell him I will sell none of my slaves; not the least little *négrillon*. Drive him from the place with the shot-gun. Don't be afraid to use the shot-gun, Alcibiade,—when I am asleep,—if he comes."

Esmée and Bartner forgot that there was such a thing as time, and that it was passing. There were no more calls of "Alcibiade, *mon fils!*" As the sun dipped lower and lower in the west, its light was creeping, creeping up and illuming the still body of Monsieur Jean Ba. It lighted his waxen hands, folded so placidly in his lap; it touched his shrunken bosom. When it reached his face, another brightness had come there before it,—the glory of a quiet and peaceful death.

Bartner remained over night, of course, to add what assistance he could to that which kindly neighbors offered.

In the early morning, before taking his departure, he was permitted to see Esmée. She was overcome with sorrow, which he could hardly hope to assuage, even with the keen sympathy which he felt.

"And may I be permitted to ask, Mademoiselle, what will be your plans for the future?"

"Oh," she moaned, "I cannot any longer remain upon the ole plantation, which would not be home without grandpère. I suppose I shall go to live in New Orleans with my *tante* Clémentine." The last was spoken in the depths of her handkerchief.

Bartner's heart bounded at this intelligence in a manner which he could not but feel was one of unbecoming levity. He pressed her disengaged hand warmly, and went away.

The sun was again shining brightly, but the morning was crisp and cool; a thin wafer of ice covered what had yesterday been pools or water in the road. Bartner buttoned his coat about him closely. The shrill whistles of steam cotton-gins sounded here and there. One or two shivering negroes were in the field gathering what shreds of cotton were left on the dry, naked stalks. The horses snorted with satisfaction, and their strong hoof-beats rang out against the hard ground.

"Urge the horses," Bartner said; "they've had a good rest and we want to push on to Natchitoches."

"You right, suh. We done los' a whole blesse' day,—a plumb day."

"Why, so we have," said Bartner, "I had n't thought of it."

A Rude Awakening

"Take de do' an' go! You year me? Take de do'!"
Lolotte's brown eyes flamed. Her small frame quivered. She stood with her back turned to a meagre supper-table, as if to guard it from the man who had just entered the cabin. She pointed toward the door, to order him from the house.

"You mighty cross to-night, Lolotte. You mus' got up wid de wrong foot to's mo'nin'. *Hein*, Veveste? *hein*, Jacques, w'at you say?"

The two small urchins who sat at table giggled in sympathy with their father's evident good humor.

"I'm we' out, me!" the girl exclaimed, desperately, as she let her arms fall limp at her side. "Work, work! Fu w'at? Fu feed de lazies' man in Natchitoches pa'ish."

"Now, Lolotte, you think w'at you say in'," expostulated her father. "Sylveste Bordon don' ax nobody to feed 'im."

"W'en you brought a poun' of suga in de house?" his daughter retorted hotly, "or a poun' of coffee? W'en did you brought a piece o' meat home, you? An' Nonomme all de time sick. Co'n bread an' po'k, dat's good fu Veveste an' me an' Jacques; but Nonomme? no!"

She turned as if choking, and cut into the round, soggy "pone" of corn bread which was the main feature of the scanty supper.

"Po' li'le Nonomme; we mus' fine some'in' to break dat fevah. You want to kill a chicken once a w'ile fu Nonomme, Lolotte." He calmly seated himself at the table.

"Did n' I done put de las' roostah in de pot?" she cried with exasperation. "Now you come axen me fu kill de hen'! W'ere I goen to fine aigg' to trade wid, w'en de hen' be gone? Is I got one picayune in de house fu trade wid, me?"

"Papa," piped the young Jacques, "w'at dat I yeard you drive in de yard, w'ile go?"

"Dat's it! W'en Lolotte would n' been talken' so fas', I could tole you 'bout dat job I got fu to-morrow. Dat was Joe Duplan's team of mule' an' wagon, wid t'ree bale' of cotton, w'at you yaird. I got to go soon in de mo'nin' wid dat load to de landin'. An' a man mus' eat w'at got to work; dat's sho."

Lolotte's bare brown feet made no sound upon the rough boards as she entered the room where Nonomme lay sick and sleeping. She lifted the coarse mosquito net from about him, sat down in the clumsy chair by the bedside, and began gently to fan the slumbering child.

Dusk was falling rapidly, as it does in the South. Lolotte's eyes grew round and big, as she watched the moon creep up from branch to branch of the moss-draped live-oak just outside her window. Presently the weary girl slept as profoundly as Nonomme. A little dog sneaked into the room, and socially licked her bare feet. The touch, moist and warm, awakened Lolotte.

The cabin was dark and quiet. Nonomme was crying softly, because the mosquitoes were biting him. In the room beyond, old Sylveste and the others slept. When Lolotte had quieted the child, she went outside to get a pail of cool, fresh water at the cistern. Then she crept into bed beside Nonomme, who slept again.

Lolotte's dreams that night pictured her father returning from work, and bringing luscious oranges home in his pocket for the sick child.

When at the very break of day she heard him astir in his room, a certain comfort stole into her heart. She lay and listened to the faint noises of his preparations to go out. When he had quitted the house, she waited to hear him drive the wagon from the yard.

She waited long, but heard no sound of horse's tread or wagon-wheel. Anxious, she went to the cabin door and looked out. The big mules were still where they had been fastened the night before. The wagon was there, too.

Her heart sank. She looked quickly along the low rafters supporting the roof of the narrow porch to where her father's fishing pole and pail always hung. Both were gone.

"'T ain' no use, 't ain' no use," she said, as she turned into the house with a look of something like anguish in her eyes.

When the spare breakfast was eaten and the dishes cleared away, Lolotte turned with resolute mien to the two little brothers.

"Veveste," she said to the older, "go see if dey got co'n in dat wagon fu feed deni mule'."

"Yes, dey got co'n. Papa done feed 'em, fur I see de co'n-cob in de trough, me."

"Den you goen he'p me hitch dem mule' to de wagon. Jacques, go down de lane an' ax Aunt Minty if she come set wid Nonomme w'ile I go drive dem mule' to de landin'."

Lolotte had evidently determined to undertake her father's work. Nothing could dissuade her; neither the children's astonishment nor

Aunt Minty's scathing disapproval. The fat black negress came laboring into the yard just as Lolotte mounted upon the wagon.

"Git down f'om dah, chile! Is you plumb crazy?" she exclaimed.

"No, I ain't crazy; I'm hungry, Aunt Minty. We all hungry. Somebody got fur work in dis fam'ly."

"Dat ain't no work fur a gal w'at ain't bar' seventeen year ole; drivin' Marse Duplan's mules! W'at I gwine tell yo' pa?"

"Fu me, you kin tell 'im w'at you want. But you watch Nonomme. I done cook his rice an' set it 'side."

"Don't you bodda," replied Aunt Minty; "I got somepin heah fur my boy. I gwine 'ten' to him."

Lolotte had seen Aunt Minty put something out of sight when she came up, and made her produce it. It was a heavy fowl.

"Sence w'en you start raisin' Brahma chicken', you?" Lolotte asked mistrustfully.

"My, but you is a cu'ious somebody! Ev'ything w'at got fedders on its laigs is Brahma chicken wid you. Dis heah ole hen"—

"All de same, you don't got fur give dat chicken to eat to Nonomme. You don't got fur cook 'im in my house."

Aunt Minty, unheeding, turned to the house with blustering inquiry for her boy, while Lolotte drove away with great clatter.

She knew, notwithstanding her injunction, that the chicken would be cooked and eaten. Maybe she herself would partake of it when she came back, if hunger drove her too sharply.

"Nax' thing I'm goen be one rogue," she muttered; and the tears gathered and fell one by one upon her cheeks.

"It *do* look like one Brahma, Aunt Mint," remarked the small and weazened Jacques, as he watched the woman picking the lusty fowl.

"How ole is you?" was her quiet retort.

"I don' know, me."

"Den if you don't know dat much, you betta keep yo' mouf shet, boy."

Then silence fell, but for a monotonous chant which the woman droned as she worked. Jacques opened his lips once more.

"It *do* look like one o' Ma'me Duplan' Brahma, Aunt Mint."

"Yonda, whar I come f'om, befo' de wah"—

"Ole Kaintuck, Aunt Mint?"

"Ole Kaintuck."

"Dat ain't one country like dis yere, Aunt Mint?"

"You mighty right, chile, dat ain't no sech kentry as dis heah. Yonda, in Kaintuck, w'en boys says de word 'Brahma chicken,' we takes an' gags 'em, an' ties dar han's behines 'em, an' fo'ces 'em ter stan' up watchin' folks settin' down eatin' chicken soup."

Jacques passed the back of his hand across his mouth; but lest the act should not place sufficient seal upon it; he prudently stole away to go and sit beside Nonomme, and wait there as patiently as he could the coming feast.

And what a treat it was! The luscious soup,—a great pot of it,—golden yellow, thickened with the flaky rice that Lolotte had set carefully on the shelf. Each mouthful of it seemed to carry fresh blood into the veins and a new brightness into the eyes of the hungry children who ate of it.

And that was not all. The day brought abundance with it. Their father came home with glistening perch and trout that Aunt Minty broiled deliciously over glowing embers, and basted with the rich chicken fat.

"You see," explained old Sylveste, "w'en I git up to 's mo'nin' an' see it was cloudy, I say to me, 'Sylveste, w'en you go wid dat cotton, rememba you got no tarpaulin. Maybe it rain, an' de cotton was spoil. Betta you go yonda to Lafirme Lake, w'ere de trout was bitin' fas'er 'an mosquito, an' so you git a good mess fur de chil'en.' Lolotte—w'at she goen do yonda? You ought stop Lolotte, Aunt Minty, w'en you see w'at she was want to do."

"Did n' I try to stop 'er? Did n' I ax 'er, 'W'at I gwine tell yo' pa?' An' she 'low, 'Tell 'im to go hang hisse'f, de triflind ole rapscallion! I's de one w'at's runnin' dis heah fambly!'"

"Dat don' soun' like Lolotte, Aunt Minty; you mus' yaird 'er crooked; *hein*, Nonomme?"

The quizzical look in his good-natured features was irresistible. Nonomme fairly shook with merriment.

"My head feel so good," he declared. "I wish Lolotte would come, so I could tole 'er." And he turned in his bed to look down the long, dusty lane, with the hope of seeing her appear as he had watched her go, sitting on one of the cotton bales and guiding the mules.

But no one came all through the hot morning. Only at noon a broad-shouldered young negro appeared in view riding through the dust. When he had dismounted at the cabin door, he stood leaning a shoulder lazily against the jamb.

"Well, heah you is," he grumbled, addressing Sylveste with no mark of respect.

"Heah you is, settin' down like comp'ny, an' Marse Joe yonda sont me see if you was dead."

"Joe Duplan boun' to have his joke, him," said Sylveste, smiling uneasily.

"Maybe it look like a joke to you, but 't aint no joke to him, man, to have one o' his wagons smoshed to kindlin', an' his bes' team tearin' t'rough de country. You don't want to let 'im lay ban's on you, joke o' no joke."

"*Malédiction!*" howled Sylveste, as he staggered to his feet. He stood for one instant irresolute; then he lurched past the man and ran wildly down the lane. He might have taken the horse that was there, but he went tottering on afoot, a frightened look in his eyes, as if his soul gazed upon an inward picture that was horrible.

The road to the landing was little used. As Sylveste went he could readily trace the marks of Lolotte's wagon-wheels. For some distance they went straight along the road. Then they made a track as if a madman had directed their course, over stump and hillock, tearing the bushes and barking the trees on either side.

At each new turn Sylveste expected to find Lolotte stretched senseless upon the ground, but, there was never a sign of her.

At last he reached the landing, which was a dreary spot, slanting down to the river and partly cleared to afford room for what desultory freight might be left there from time to time. There were the wagon-tracks, clean down to the river's edge and partly in the water, where they made a sharp and senseless turn. But Sylveste found no trace of his girl.

"Lolotte!" the old man cried out into the stillness. "Lolotte, *ma fille*, Lolotte!" But no answer came; no sound but the echo of his own voice, and the soft splash of the red water that lapped his feet.

He looked down at it, sick with anguish and apprehension.

Lolotte had disappeared as completely as if the earth had opened and swallowed her. After a few days it became the common belief that the girl had been drowned. It was thought that she must have been hurled from the wagon into the water during the sharp turn that the wheel-tracks indicated, and carried away by the rapid current.

During the days of search, old Sylveste's excitement kept him up. When it was over, an apathetic despair seemed to settle upon him.

Madame Duplan, moved by sympathy, had taken the little four-year-old Nonomme to the plantation Les Chêniers, where the child was awed by the beauty and comfort of things that surrounded him there. He thought always that Lolotte would come back, and watched for her every day; for they did not tell him the sad tidings of her loss.

The other two boys were placed in the temporary care of Aunt Minty; and old Sylveste roamed like a persecuted being through the country. He who had been a type of indolent content and repose had changed to a restless spirit.

When he thought to eat, it was in some humble negro cabin that he stopped to ask for food, which was never denied him. His grief had clothed him with a dignity that imposed respect.

One morning very early he appeared before the planter with a disheveled and hunted look.

"M'sieur Duplan," he said, holding his hat in his hand and looking away into vacancy, "I been try ev'thing. I been try settin' down still on de sto' gall'ry. I been walk, I been run; 't ain' no use. Dey got al'ays some'in' w'at push me. I go fishin', an' it's some'in' w'at push me worser 'an ever. By gracious! M'sieur Duplan, gi' me some work!"

The planter gave him at once a plow in hand, and no plow on the whole plantation dug so deep as that one, nor so fast. Sylveste was the first in the field, as he was the last one there. From dawn to nightfall he worked, and after, till his limbs refused to do his bidding.

People came to wonder, and the negroes began to whisper hints of demoniacal possession.

When Mr. Duplan gave careful thought to the subject of Lolotte's mysterious disappearance, an idea came to him. But so fearful was he to arouse false hopes in the breasts of those who grieved for the girl that to no one did he impart his suspicions save to his wife. It was on the eve of a business trip to New Orleans that he told her what he thought, or what he hoped rather.

Upon his return, which happened not many days later, he went out to where old Sylveste was toiling in the field with frenzied energy.

"Sylveste," said the planter, quietly, when he had stood a moment watching the man at work, "have you given up all hope of hearing from your daughter?"

"I don' know, me; I don' know. Le' me work, M'sieur Duplan."

"For my part, I believe the child is alive."

"You b'lieve dat, you?" His rugged face was pitiful in its imploring lines.

"I know it," Mr. Duplan muttered, as calmly as he could. "Hold up! Steady yourself, man! Come; come with me to the house. There is some one there who knows it, too; some one who has seen her."

The room into which the planter led the old man was big, cool, beautiful, and sweet with the delicate odor of flowers. It was shady, too, for the shutters were half closed; but not so darkened but Sylveste could at once see Lolotte, seated in a big wicker chair.

She was almost as white as the gown she wore. Her neatly shod feet rested upon a cushion, and her black hair, that had been closely cut, was beginning to make little rings about her temples.

"Aie!" he cried sharply, at sight of her, grasping his seamed throat as he did so. Then he laughed like a madman, and then he sobbed.

He only sobbed, kneeling upon the floor beside her, kissing her knees and her hands, that sought his. Little Nonomme was close to her, with a health flush creeping into his cheek. Veveste and Jacques were there, and rather awed by the mystery and grandeur of everything.

"W'ere'bouts you find her, M'sieur Duplan?" Sylveste asked, when the first flush of his joy had spent itself, and he was wiping his eyes with his rough cotton shirt sleeve.

"M'sieur Duplan find me 'way yonda to de city, papa, in de hospital," spoke Lolotte, before the planter could steady his voice to reply. "I did n' know who ev'ybody was, me. I did n' know me, myse'f, tell I tu'n roun' one day an' see M'sieur Duplan, w'at stan'en dere."

"You was boun' to know M'sieur Duplan, Lolotte," laughed Sylveste, like a child.

"Yes, an' I know right 'way how dem mule was git frighten' w'en de boat w'istle fu stop, an' pitch me plumb on de groun'. An' I remamba it was one *mulâtresse* w'at call herse'f one chembamed, all de time aside me."

"You must not talk too much, Lolotte," interposed Madame Duplan, coming to place her hand with gentle solicitude upon the girl's forehead, and to feel how her pulse beat.

Then to save the child further effort of speech, she herself related how the boat had stopped at this lonely landing to take on a load of cotton-seed. Lolotte had been found stretched insensible by the river, fallen apparently from the clouds, and had been taken on board.

The boat had changed its course into other waters after that trip, and had not returned to Duplan's Landing. Those who had tended Lolotte and left her at the hospital supposed, no doubt, that she would make known her identity in time, and they had troubled themselves no further about her.

"An' dah you is!" almost shouted aunt Minty, whose black face gleamed in the doorway; "dah you is, settin' down, lookin' jis' like w'ite folks!"

KATE CHOPIN

"Ain't I always was w'ite folks, Aunt Mint?" smiled Lolotte, feebly.

"G'long, chile. You knows me. I don' mean no harm."

"And now, Sylveste," said Mr. Duplan, as he rose and started to walk the floor, with hands in his pockets, "listen to me. It will be a long time before Lolotte is strong again. Aunt Minty is going to look after things for you till the child is fully recovered. But what I want to say is this: I shall trust these children into your hands once more, and I want you never to forget again that you are their father—do you hear?—that you are a man!"

Old Sylveste stood with his hand in Lolotte's, who rubbed it lovingly against her cheek.

"By gracious! M'sieur Duplan," he answered, "w'en God want to he'p me, I'm goen try my bes'!"

The Bênitous' Slave

O ld Uncle Oswald believed he belonged to the Bênitous, and there was no getting the notion out of his head. Monsieur tried every way, for there was no sense in it. Why, it must have been fifty years since the Bênitous owned him. He had belonged to others since, and had later been freed. Beside, there was not a Bênitou left in the parish now, except one rather delicate woman, who lived with her little daughter in a corner of Natchitoches town, and constructed "fashionable millinery." The family had dispersed, and almost vanished, and the plantation as well had lost its identity.

But that made no difference to Uncle Oswald. He was always running away from Monsieur—who kept him out of pure kindness—and trying to get back to those Bênitous.

More than that, he was constantly getting injured in such attempts. Once he fell into the bayou and was nearly drowned. Again he barely escaped being run down by an engine. But another time, when he had been lost two days, and finally discovered in an unconscious and half-dead condition in the woods, Monsieur and Doctor Bonfils reluctantly decided that it was time to "do something" with the old man.

So, one sunny spring morning, Monsieur took Uncle Oswald in the buggy, and drove over to Natchitoches with him, intending to take the evening train for the institution in which the poor creature was to be cared for.

It was quite early in the afternoon when they reached town, and Monsieur found himself with several hours to dispose of before train-time. He tied his horses in front of the hotel—the quaintest old stuccoed house, too absurdly unlike a "hotel" for anything—and entered. But he left Uncle Oswald seated upon a shaded bench just within the yard.

There were people occasionally coming in and going out; but no one took the smallest notice of the old negro drowsing over the cane that he held between his knees. The sight was common in Natchitoches.

One who passed in was a little girl about twelve, with dark, kind eyes, and daintily carrying a parcel. She was dressed in blue calico, and wore a stiff white sun-bonnet, extinguisher fashion, over her brown curls.

Just as she passed Uncle Oswald again, on her way out, the old man, half asleep, let fall his cane. She picked it up and handed it back to him, as any nice child would have done.

"Oh, thankee, thankee, missy," stammered Uncle Oswald, all confused at being waited upon by this little lady. "You is a putty li'le gal. W'at's yo' name, honey?"

"My name's Susanne; Susanne Bênitou," replied the girl.

Instantly the old negro stumbled to his feet. Without a moment's hesitancy he followed the little one out through the gate, down the street, and around the corner.

It was an hour later that Monsieur, after a distracted search, found him standing upon the gallery of the tiny house in which Madame Bênitou kept "fashionable millinery."

Mother and daughter were sorely perplexed to comprehend the intentions of the venerable servitor, who stood, hat in hand, persistently awaiting their orders.

Monsieur understood and appreciated the situation at once, and he has prevailed upon Madame Bênitou to accept the gratuitous services of Uncle Oswald for the sake of the old darky's own safety and happiness.

Uncle Oswald never tries to run away now. He chops wood and hauls water. He cheerfully and faithfully bears the parcels that Susanne used to carry; and makes an excellent cup of black coffee.

I met the old man the other day in Natchitoches, contentedly stumbling down St. Denis street with a basket of figs that some one was sending to his mistress. I asked him his name.

"My name's Oswal', Madam; Oswal'—dat's my name. I b'longs to de Bênitous," and some one told me his story then.

Désirée's Baby

As the day was pleasant, Madame Valmondé drove over to L'Abri to see Désirée and the baby.

It made her laugh to think of Désirée with a baby. Why, it seemed but yesterday that Désirée was little more than a baby herself; when Monsieur in riding through the gateway of Valmondé had found her lying asleep in the shadow of the big stone pillar.

The little one awoke in his arms and began to cry for "Dada." That was as much as she could do or say. Some people thought she might have strayed there of her own accord, for she was of the toddling age. The prevailing belief was that she had been purposely left by a party of Texans, whose canvas-covered wagon, late in the day, had crossed the ferry that Coton Maïs kept, just below the plantation. In time Madame Valmondé abandoned every speculation but the one that Désirée had been sent to her by a beneficent Providence to be the child of her affection, seeing that she was without child of the flesh. For the girl grew to be beautiful and gentle, affectionate and sincere,—the idol of Valmondé.

It was no wonder, when she stood one day against the stone pillar in whose shadow she had lain asleep, eighteen years before, that Armand Aubigny riding by and seeing her there, had fallen in love with her. That was the way all the Aubignys fell in love, as if struck by a pistol shot. The wonder was that he had not loved her before; for he had known her since his father brought him home from Paris, a boy of eight, after his mother died there. The passion that awoke in him that day, when he saw her at the gate, swept along like an avalanche, or like a prairie fire, or like anything that drives headlong over all obstacles.

Monsieur Valmondé grew practical and wanted things well considered: that is, the girl's obscure origin. Armand looked into her eyes and did not care. He was reminded that she was nameless. What did it matter about a name when he could give her one of the oldest and proudest in Louisiana? He ordered the corbeille from Paris, and contained himself with what patience he could until it arrived; then they were married.

Madame Valmondé had not seen Désirée and the baby for four weeks. When she reached L'Abri she shuddered at the first sight of it, as she always did. It was a sad looking place, which for many years had not known the gentle presence of a mistress, old Monsieur Aubigny having married and buried his wife in France, and she having loved her own land too well ever to leave it. The roof came down steep and black like a cowl, reaching out beyond the wide galleries that encircled the yellow stuccoed house. Big, solemn oaks grew close to it, and their thick-leaved, far-reaching branches shadowed it like a pall. Young Aubigny's rule was a strict one, too, and under it his negroes had forgotten how to be gay, as they had been during the old master's easy-going and indulgent lifetime.

The young mother was recovering slowly, and lay full length, in her soft white muslins and laces, upon a couch. The baby was beside her, upon her arm, where he had fallen asleep, at her breast. The yellow nurse woman sat beside a window fanning herself.

Madame Valmondé bent her portly figure over Désirée and kissed her, holding her an instant tenderly in her arms. Then she turned to the child.

"This is not the baby!" she exclaimed, in startled tones. French was the language spoken at Valmondé in those days.

"I knew you would be astonished," laughed Désirée, "at the way he has grown. The little *cochon de lait!* Look at his legs, mamma, and his hands and finger-nails,—real finger-nails. Zandrine had to cut them this morning. Is n't it true, Zandrine?"

The woman bowed her turbaned head majestically, "Mais si, Madame."

"And the way he cries," went on Désirée, "is deafening. Armand heard him the other day as far away as La Blanche's cabin."

Madame Valmondé had never removed her eyes from the child. She lifted it and walked with it over to the window that was lightest. She scanned the baby narrowly, then looked as searchingly at Zandrine, whose face was burned to gaze across the fields.

"Yes, the child has grown, has changed;" said Madame Valmondé, slowly, as she replaced it beside its mother. "What does Armand say?"

Désirée's face became suffused with a glow that was happiness itself.

"Oh, Armand is the proudest father in the parish, I believe, chiefly because it is a boy, to bear his name; though he says not,—that he would have loved a girl as well. But I know it is n't true. I know he says that to please me. And mamma," she added, drawing Madame Valmondé's head down to her, and speaking in a whisper, "he has n't punished one of them—not one of them—since baby is born. Even Négrillon, who pretended to have burnt his leg that he might rest from work—he only, laughed, and said Négrillon was a great scamp. Oh, mamma, I'm so happy; it frightens me."

What Désirée said was true. Marriage, and later the birth of his son, had softened Armand Aubigny's imperious and exacting nature greatly. This was what made the gentle Désirée so happy, for she loved him desperately. When he frowned she trembled, but loved him. When he smiled, she asked no greater blessing of God. But Armand's dark, handsome face had not often been disfigured by frowns since the day he fell in love with her.

When the baby was about three months old, Désirée awoke one day to the conviction that there was something in the air menacing her peace. It was at first too subtle to grasp. It had only been a disquieting suggestion; an air of mystery among the blacks; unexpected visits from far-off neighbors who could hardly account for their coming. Then a strange, an awful change in her husband's manner, which she dared not ask him to explain. When he spoke to her, it was with averted eyes, from which the old love-light seemed to have gone out. He absented himself from home; and when there, avoided her presence and that of her child, without excuse. And the very spirit of Satan seemed suddenly to take hold of him in his dealings with the slaves. Désirée was miserable enough to die.

She sat in her room, one hot afternoon, in her *peignoir*, listlessly drawing through her fingers the strands of her long, silky brown hair that hung about her shoulders. The baby, half naked, lay asleep upon her own great mahogany bed, that was like a sumptuous throne, with its satin-lined half-canopy. One of La Blanche's little quadroon boys—half naked too—stood fanning the child slowly with a fan of peacock feathers. Désirée's eyes had been fixed absently and sadly upon the baby, while she was striving to penetrate the threatening mist that she felt closing about her. She looked from her child to the boy who stood beside him, and back again; over and over. "Ah!" It was a cry that she could not help; which she was not conscious of having uttered. The blood turned like ice in her veins, and a clammy moisture gathered upon her face.

She tried to speak to the little quadroon boy; but no sound would come, at first. When he heard his name uttered, he looked up, and his mistress was pointing to the door. He laid aside the great, soft fan, and obediently stole away, over the polished floor, on his bare tiptoes.

She stayed motionless, with gaze riveted upon her child, and her face the picture of fright.

Presently her husband entered the room, and without noticing her, went to a table and began to search among some papers which covered it.

"Armand," she called to him, in a voice which must have stabbed him, if he was human. But he did not notice. "Armand," she said again. Then she rose and tottered towards him. "Armand," she panted once more, clutching his arm, "look at our child. What does it mean? tell me."

He coldly but gently loosened her fingers from about his arm and thrust the hand away from him. "Tell me what it means!" she cried despairingly.

"It means," he answered lightly, "that the child is not white; it means that you are not white."

A quick conception of all that this accusation meant for her nerved her with unwonted courage to deny it. "It is a lie; it is not true, I am white! Look at my hair, it is brown; and my eyes are gray, Armand, you know they are gray. And my skin is fair," seizing his wrist. "Look at my hand; whiter than yours, Armand," she laughed hysterically.

"As white as La Blanche's," he returned cruelly; and went away leaving her alone with their child.

When she could hold a pen in her hand, she sent a despairing letter to Madame Valmondé.

"My mother, they tell me I am not white. Armand has told me I am not white. For God's sake tell them it is not true. You must know it is not true. I shall die. I must die. I cannot be so unhappy, and live.".

The answer that came was as brief:

"My own Désirée: Come home to Valmondé; back to your mother who loves you. Come with your child."

When the letter reached Désirée she went with it to her husband's study, and laid it open upon the desk before which he sat. She was like a stone image: silent, white, motionless after she placed it there.

In silence he ran his cold eyes over the written words. He said nothing. "Shall I go, Armand?" she asked in tones sharp with agonized suspense.

"Yes, go."

"Do you want me to go?"

"Yes, I want you to go."

He thought Almighty God had dealt cruelly and unjustly with him; and felt, somehow, that he was paying Him back in kind when he stabbed thus into his wife's soul. Moreover he no longer loved her, because of the unconscious injury she had brought upon his home and his name.

She turned away like one stunned by a blow, and walked slowly towards the door, hoping he would call her back.

"Good-by, Armand," she moaned.

He did not answer her. That was his last blow at fate.

Désirée went in search of her child. Zandrine was pacing the sombre gallery with it. She took the little one from the nurse's arms with no word of explanation, and descending the steps, walked away, under the live-oak branches.

It was an October afternoon; the sun was just sinking. Out in the still fields the negroes were picking cotton.

Désirée had not changed the thin white garment nor the slippers which she wore. Her hair was uncovered and the sun's rays brought a golden gleam from its brown meshes. She did not take the broad, beaten road which led to the far-off plantation of Valmondé. She walked across a deserted field, where the stubble bruised her tender feet, so delicately shod, and tore her thin gown to shreds.

She disappeared among the reeds and willows that grew thick along the banks of the deep, sluggish bayou; and she did not come back again.

SOME WEEKS LATER THERE WAS a curious scene enacted at L'Abri. In the centre of the smoothly swept back yard was a great bonfire. Armand Aubigny sat in the wide hall-way that commanded a view of the spectacle; and it was he who dealt out to a half dozen negroes the material which kept this fire ablaze.

A graceful cradle of willow, with all its dainty furbishings, was laid upon the pyre, which had already been fed with the richness of a priceless *layette*. Then there were silk gowns, and velvet and satin ones added to these; laces, too, and embroideries; bonnets and gloves; for the *corbeille* had been of rare quality.

The last thing to go was a tiny bundle of letters; innocent little scribblings that Désirée had sent to him during the days of their espousal. There was the remnant of one back in the drawer from which he took them. But it was not Désirée's; it was part of an old letter from his mother to his father. He read it. She was thanking God for the blessing of her husband's love:—

"But, above all," she wrote, "night and day, I thank the good God for having so arranged our lives that our dear Armand will never know that his mother, who adores him, belongs to the race that is cursed with the brand of slavery."

A Turkey Hunt

Three of Madame's finest bronze turkeys were missing from the brood. It was nearing Christmas, and that was the reason, perhaps, that even Monsieur grew agitated when the discovery was made. The news was brought to the house by Séverin's boy, who had seen the troop at noon a half mile up the bayou three short. Others reported the deficiency as even greater. So, at about two in the afternoon, though a cold drizzle had begun to fall, popular feeling in the matter was so strong that all the household forces turned out to search for the missing gobblers.

Alice, the housemaid, went down the river, and Polisson the yard-boy, went up the bayou. Others crossed the fields, and Artemise was rather vaguely instructed to "go look too."

Artemise is in some respects an extraordinary person. In age she's anywhere between 10 and 15, with a head not unlike in shape and appearance to a dark chocolate-colored Easter-egg. She talks most wholly in monosyllables, and has big round glassy eyes, which she fixes upon one with the placid gaze of an Egyptian sphinx.

The morning after my arrival at the plantation, I was awakened by the rattling of cups at my bedside. It was Artemise with the early coffee.

"Is it cold out?" I asked by way of conversation, as I sipped the tiny cup of ink-black coffee.

"Ya, 'm."

"Where do you sleep, Artemise?" I further inquired, with the same intention as before.

"In uh hole," was precisely what she said, with a pump-like motion of the arm that she habitually uses to indicate a locality. What she meant was that she slept in the hall.

Again, another time, she came with an armful of wood, and having deposited it upon the hearth, turn to stare fixedly at me, with folded hands.

"Did Madame send you to build a fire, Artemise?" I hastened to ask, feeling uncomfortable under the look.

"Ya, 'm."

"Very well; make it."

"Matches!" was all she said.

There happened to be no matches in my room, and she evidently considered that all personal responsibility ceased in face of this first and not very serious obstacle. Pages might be told of her unfathomable ways; but to the turkey hunt.

All afternoon the searching party kept returning, singly and in couples, and in a more or less bedraggled condition. All brought unfavorable reports. Nothing could be seen of the missing fowls. Artemise had been absent probably an hour when she glided into the hall where the family was assembled, an stood with crossed hands and contemplative air beside the fire. We could see by the benign expression of her countenance that she possibly had information to give, if any inducement were offered her in the shape of a question.

"Have you found the turkeys, Artemise?" Madame hastened to ask.

"Ya, 'm."

"You Artemise!" shouted Aunt Florindy, the cook, who was passing through the hall with a batch of newly baked light bread. "She's a-lyin', mist'ess, if dey ever was! *You* foun' dem turkeys?" upon the child. "Whar was you at, de whole blesse' time? Warn't you stan'in' plank up agin de back o' de hen-'ous'? Never budged a inch? Don't jaw me down, gal; don't jaw me!" Artemise was only gazing at Aunt Florindy with unruffled calm. "I warn't gwine tell on 'er, but arter dat untroof, I boun' to."

"Let her alone, Aunt Florindy," Madame interfered. "Where are the turkeys, Artemise?"

"Yon'a," she simply articulated, bringing the pump-handle motion of her arm into play.

"Where 'yonder'?" Madame demanded, a little impatiently.

"In uh hen-'ous'!"

Sure enough! The three missing turkeys had been accidentally locked up in the morning when the chickens were fed.

Artemise, for some unknown reason, had hidden herself during the search behind the hen-house, and had heard their muffled gobble.

Madame Célestin's Divorce

Madame Célestin always wore a neat and snugly fitting calico wrapper when she went out in the morning to sweep her small gallery. Lawyer Paxton thought she looked very pretty in the gray one that was made with a graceful Watteau fold at the back: and with which she invariably wore a bow of pink ribbon at the throat. She was always sweeping her gallery when lawyer Paxton passed by in the morning on his way to his office in St. Denis Street.

Sometimes he stopped and leaned over the fence to say good-morning at his ease; to criticise or admire her rosebushes; or, when he had time enough, to hear what she had to say. Madame Célestin usually had a good deal to say. She would gather up the train of her calico wrapper in one hand, and balancing the broom gracefully in the other, would go tripping down to where the lawyer leaned, as comfortably as he could, over her picket fence.

Of course she had talked to him of her troubles. Every one knew Madame Célestin's troubles.

"Really, madame," he told her once, in his deliberate, calculating, lawyer—tone, "it's more than human nature—woman's nature—should be called upon to endure. Here you are, working your fingers off"—she glanced down at two rosy finger-tips that showed through the rents in her baggy doe-skin gloves—"taking in sewing; giving music lessons; doing God knows what in the way of manual labor to support yourself and those two little ones"—Madame Célestin's pretty face beamed with satisfaction at this enumeration of her trials.

"You right, Judge. Not a picayune, not one, not one, have I lay my eyes on in the pas' fo' months that I can say Célestin give it to me or sen' it to me."

"The scoundrel!" muttered lawyer Paxton in his beard.

"An' *pourtant*," she resumed, "they say he's making money down roun' Alexandria w'en he wants to work."

"I dare say you have n't seen him for months?" suggested the lawyer.

"It's good six month' since I see a sight of Célestin," she admitted.

"That's it, that's what I say; he has practically deserted you; fails to support you. It wouldn't surprise me a bit to learn that he has ill treated you."

"Well, you know, Judge," with an evasive cough, "a man that drinks—w'at can you expec'? An' if you would know the promises he has made me! Ah, if I had as many dolla' as I had promise from Célestin, I would n' have to work, *je vous garantis*."

"And in my opinion, madame, you would be a foolish woman to endure it longer, when the divorce court is there to offer you redress."

"You spoke about that befo', Judge; I'm goin' think about that divo'ce. I believe you right."

Madame Célestin thought about the divorce and talked about it, too; and lawyer Paxton grew deeply interested in the theme.

"You know, about that divo'ce, Judge," Madame Célestin was waiting for him that morning, "I been talking to my family an' my frien's, an' it's me that tells you, they all plumb agains' that divo'ce."

"Certainly, to be sure; that's to be expected, madame, in this community of Creoles. I warned you that you would meet with opposition, and would have to face it and brave it."

"Oh, don't fear, I'm going to face it! Maman says it's a disgrace like it's neva been in the family. But it's good for Maman to talk, her. W'at trouble she ever had? She says I mus' go by all means consult with Père Duchéron—it's my confessor, you undastan'—Well, I'll go, Judge, to please Maman. But all the confessor' in the worl' ent goin' make me put up with that conduc' of Célestin any longa."

A day or two later, she was there waiting for him again. "You know, Judge, about that divo'ce."

"Yes, yes," responded the lawyer, well pleased to trace a new determination in her brown eyes and in the curves of her pretty mouth. "I suppose you saw Père Duchéron and had to brave it out with him, too."

"Oh, fo' that, a perfec' sermon, I assho you. A talk of giving scandal an' bad example that I thought would neva en'! He says, fo' him, he wash' his hands; I mus' go see the bishop."

"You won't let the bishop dissuade you, I trust," stammered the lawyer more anxiously than he could well understand.

"You don't know me yet, Judge," laughed Madame Célestin with a turn of the head and a flirt of the broom which indicated that the interview was at an end.

"Well, Madame Célestin! And the bishop!" Lawyer Paxton was standing there holding to a couple of the shaky pickets. She had not seen him. "Oh, it's you, Judge?" and she hastened towards him with an *empressement* that could not but have been flattering.

"Yes, I saw Monseigneur," she began. The lawyer had already gathered from her expressive countenance that she had not wavered in her determination. "Ah, he's a eloquent man. It's not a mo' eloquent man in Natchitoches parish. I was fo'ced to cry, the way he talked to me about my troubles; how he undastan's them, an' feels for me. It would move even you, Judge, to hear how he talk' about that step I want to take; its danga, its temptation. How it is the duty of a Catholic to stan' everything till the las' extreme. An' that life of retirement an' self-denial I would have to lead,—he tole me all that."

"But he has n't turned you from your resolve, I see," laughed the lawyer complacently.

"For that, no," she returned emphatically. "The bishop don't know w'at it is to be married to a man like Célestin, an' have to endu' that conduc' like I have to endu' it. The Pope himse'f can't make me stan' that any longer, if you say I got the right in the law to sen' Célestin sailing."

A noticeable change had come over lawyer Paxton. He discarded his work-day coat and began to wear his Sunday one to the office. He grew solicitous as to the shine of his boots, his collar, and the set of his tie. He brushed and trimmed his whiskers with a care that had not before been apparent. Then he fell into a stupid habit of dreaming as he walked the streets of the old town. It would be very good to take unto himself a wife, he dreamed. And he could dream of no other than pretty Madame Célestin filling that sweet and sacred office as she filled his thoughts, now. Old Natchitoches would not hold them comfortably, perhaps; but the world was surely wide enough to live in, outside of Natchitoches town.

His heart beat in a strangely irregular manner as he neared Madame Célestin's house one morning, and discovered her behind the rosebushes, as usual plying her broom. She had finished the gallery and steps and was sweeping the little brick walk along the edge of the violet border.

"Good-morning, Madame Célestin."

"Ah, it's you, Judge? Good-morning." He waited. She seemed to be doing the same. Then she ventured, with some hesitancy, "You know, Judge, about that divo'ce. I been thinking,—I reckon you betta neva mine about that divo'ce." She was making deep rings in the palm of her gloved hand with the end of the broom-handle, and looking at them critically. Her face seemed to the lawyer to be unusually rosy; but maybe it was only the reflection of the pink bow at the throat. "Yes, I reckon you need n' mine. You see, Judge, Célestin came home las' night. An' he's promise me on his word an' honor he's going to turn ova a new leaf."

Love on the Bon-Dieu

U pon the pleasant veranda of Père Antoine's cottage, that adjoined the church, a young girl had long been seated, awaiting his return. It was the eve of Easter Sunday, and since early afternoon the priest had been engaged in hearing the confessions of those who wished to make their Easters the following day. The girl did not seem impatient at his delay; on the contrary, it was very restful to her to lie back in the big chair she had found there, and peep through the thick curtain of vines at the people who occasionally passed along the village street.

She was slender, with a frailness that indicated lack of wholesome and plentiful nourishment. A pathetic, uneasy look was in her gray eyes, and even faintly stamped her features, which were fine and delicate. In lieu of a hat, a barege veil covered her light brown and abundant hair. She wore a coarse white cotton "josie," and a blue calico skirt that only half concealed her tattered shoes.

As she sat there, she held carefully in her lap a parcel of eggs securely fastened in a red bandana handkerchief.

Twice already a handsome, stalwart young man in quest of the priest had entered the yard, and penetrated to where she sat. At first they had exchanged the uncompromising "howdy" of strangers, and nothing more. The second time, finding the priest still absent, he hesitated to go at once. Instead, he stood upon the step, and narrowing his brown eyes, gazed beyond the river, off towards the west, where a murky streak of mist was spreading across the sun.

"It look like mo' rain," he remarked, slowly and carelessly.

"We done had 'bout 'nough," she replied, in much the same tone.

"It's no chance to thin out the cotton," he went on.

"An' the Bon-Dieu," she resumed, "it's on'y to-day you can cross him on foot."

"You live yonda on the Bon-Dieu, *donc*?" he asked, looking at her for the first time since he had spoken.

"Yas, by Nid d'Hibout, m'sieur."

Instinctive courtesy held him from questioning her further. But he seated himself on the step, evidently determined to wait there for the priest. He said no more, but sat scanning critically the steps, the porch, and pillar beside him, from which he occasionally tore away little pieces of detached wood, where it was beginning to rot at its base.

A click at the side gate that communicated with the churchyard soon announced Père Antoine's return. He came hurriedly across the garden-path, between the tall, lusty rosebushes that lined either side of it, which were now fragrant with blossoms. His long, flapping cassock added something of height to his undersized, middle-aged figure, as did the skullcap which rested securely back on his head. He saw only the young man at first, who rose at his approach.

"Well, Azenor," he called cheerily in French, extending his hand. "How is this? I expected you all the week."

"Yes, monsieur; but I knew well what you wanted with me, and I was finishing the doors for Gros-Léon's new house;" saying which, he drew back, and indicated by a motion and look that some one was present who had a prior claim upon Père Antoine's attention.—

"Ah, Lalie!" the priest exclaimed, when he had mounted to the porch, and saw her there behind the vines. "Have you been waiting here since you confessed? Surely an hour ago!"

"Yes, monsieur."

"You should rather have made some visits in the village, child."

"I am not acquainted with any one in the village," she returned.

The priest, as he spoke, had drawn a chair, and seated himself beside her, with his hands comfortably clasping his knees. He wanted to know how things were out on the bayou.

"And how is the grandmother?" he asked. "As cross and crabbed as ever? And with that"—he added reflectively—"good for ten years yet! I said only yesterday to Butrand—you know Butrand, he works on Le Blôt's Bon-Dieu place—'And that Madame Zidore: how is it with her, Butrand? I believe God has forgotten her here on earth.' 'It is n't that, your reverence,' said Butrand, 'but it's neither God nor the Devil that wants her!'" And Père Antoine laughed with a jovial frankness that took all sting of ill-nature from his very pointed remarks.

Lalie did not reply when he spoke of her grandmother; she only pressed her lips firmly together, and picked nervously at the red bandana.

"I have come to ask, Monsieur Antoine," she began, lower than she needed to speak—for Azenor had withdrawn at once to the far end of the porch—"to ask if you will give me a little scrap of paper—a piece of writing for Monsieur Chartrand at the store over there. I want new shoes and stockings for Easter, and I have brought eggs to trade for them. He says he is willing, yes, if he was sure I would bring more every week till the shoes are paid for."

With good-natured indifference, Père Antoine wrote the order that the girl desired. He was too familiar with distress to feel keenly for a girl who was able to buy Easter shoes and pay for them with eggs.

She went immediately away then, after shaking hands with the priest, and sending a quick glance of her pathetic eyes towards Azenor, who had turned when he heard her rise, and nodded when he caught the look. Through the vines he watched her cross the village street.

"How is it that you do not know Lalie, Azenor? You surely must have seen her pass your house often. It lies on her way to the Bon-Dieu."

"No, I don't know her; I have never seen her,", the young man replied, as he seated himself—after the priest—and kept his eyes absently fixed on the store across the road, where he had seen her enter.

"She is the granddaughter of that Madame Izidore"—

"What! Ma'ame Zidore whom they drove off the island last winter?"

"Yes, yes. Well, you know, they say the old woman stole wood and things,—I don't know how true it is,—and destroyed people's property out of pure malice."

"And she lives now on the Bon-Dieu?"

"Yes, on Le Blôt's place, in a perfect wreck of a cabin. You see, she gets it for nothing; not a negro on the place but has refused to live in it."

"Surely, it can't be that old abandoned hovel near the swamp, that Michon occupied ages ago?"

"That is the one, the very one."

"And the girl lives there with that old wretch?" the young man marveled.

"Old wretch to be sure, Azenor. But what can you expect from a woman who never crosses the threshold of God's house—who even tried to hinder the child doing so as well? But I went to her. I said: 'See here, Madame Zidore,'—you know it's my way to handle such people without gloves,—'you may damn your soul if you choose,' I told her, that is a privilege which we all have; but none of us has a right to imperil the salvation of another. I want to see Lalie at mass hereafter on Sundays, or you will hear from me;' and I shook my stick under her nose. Since then the child has never missed a Sunday. But she is half starved, you can see that. You saw how shabby she is—how broken her shoes are? She is at Chartrand's now, trading for new ones with those eggs she brought, poor thing! There is no doubt of her being ill-treated. Butrand says he thinks Madame Zidore even beats the child. I don't know how true it is, for no power can make her utter a word against her grandmother."

Azenor, whose face was a kind and sensitive one, had paled with distress as the priest spoke; and now at these final words he quivered as though he felt the sting of a cruel blow upon his own flesh.

But no more was said of Lalie, for Père Antoine drew the young man's attention to the carpenter-work which he wished to intrust to him. When they had talked the matter over in all its lengthy details, Azenor mounted his horse and rode away.

A moment's gallop carried him outside the village. Then came a half-mile strip along the river to cover. Then the lane to enter, in which stood his dwelling midway, upon a low, pleasant knoll.

As Azenor turned into the lane, he saw the figure of Lalie far ahead of him. Somehow he had expected to find her there, and he watched her again, as he had done through Père Antoine's vines. When she passed his house, he wondered if she would turn to look at it. But she did not. How could she know it was his? Upon reaching it himself, he did not enter the yard, but stood there motionless, his eyes always fastened upon the girl's figure. He could not see, away off there, how coarse her garments were. She seemed, through the distance that divided them, as slim and delicate as a flower-stalk. He stayed till she reached the turn of the lane and disappeared into the woods.

MASS HAD NOT YET BEGUN when Azenor tiptoed into church on Easter morning. He did not take his place with the congregation, but stood close to the holy-water font, and watched the people who entered.

Almost every girl who passed him wore a white mull, a dotted swiss, or a fresh-starched muslin at least. They were bright with ribbons that hung from their persons, and flowers that bedecked their hats. Some carried fans and cambric handkerchiefs. Most of them wore gloves, and were odorant of *poudre de riz* and nice toilet-waters; while all carried gay little baskets filled with Easter-eggs.

But there was one who came empty-handed, save for the worn prayer-book which she bore. It was Lalie, the veil upon her head, and wearing the blue print and cotton bodice which she had worn the day before.

He dipped his hand into the holy water when she came, and held it out to her, though he had not thought of doing this for the others. She touched his fingers with the tips of her own, making a slight inclination as she did so; and after a deep genuflection before the Blessed Sacrament, passed on to the side. He was not sure if she had known him. He knew she had not looked into his eyes, for he would have felt it.

He was angered against other young women who passed him, because of their flowers and ribbons, when she wore none. He himself did not care, but he feared she might, and watched her narrowly to see if she did.

But it was plain that Lalie did not care. Her face, as she seated herself, settled into the same restful lines it had worn yesterday, when she sat in Père Antoine's big chair. It seemed good to her to be there. Sometimes she looked up at the little colored panes through which the Easter sun was streaming; then at the flaming candles, like stars; or at the embowered figures of Joseph and Mary, flanking the central tabernacle which shrouded the risen Christ. Yet she liked just as well to watch the young girls in their spring freshness, or to sensuously inhale the mingled odor of flowers and incense that filled the temple.

Lalie was among the last to quit the church. When she walked down the clean pathway that led from it to the road, she looked with pleased curiosity towards the groups of men and maidens who were gayly matching their Easter-eggs under the shade of the China-berry trees.

Azenor was among them, and when he saw her coming solitary down the path, he approached her and, with a smile, extended his hat, whose crown was quite lined with the pretty colored eggs.

"You mus' of forgot to bring aiggs," he said. "Take some o' mine."

"Non, merci," she replied, flushing and drawing back.

But he urged them anew upon her. Much pleased, then, she bent her pretty head over the hat, and was evidently puzzled to make a selection among so many that were beautiful.

He picked out one for her,—a pink one, dotted with white clover-leaves.

"Yere," he said, handing it to her, "I think this is the prettied'; an' it look' strong too. I'm sho' it will break all of the res'." And he playfully held out another, half-hidden in his fist, for her to try its strength upon. But she refused to. She would not risk the ruin of her pretty egg. Then she walked away, without once having noticed that the girls, whom Azenor had left, were looking curiously at her.

When he rejoined them, he was hardly prepared for their greeting; it startled him.

"How come you talk to that girl? She's real canaille, her," was what one of them said to him.

"Who say' so? Who say she's canaille? If it's a man, I 'll smash 'is head!" he exclaimed, livid. They all laughed merrily at this.

"An' if it's a lady, Azenor? W'at you goin' to do 'bout it?" asked another, quizzingly.

"T ain' no lady. No lady would say that 'bout a po' girl, w'at she don't even know."

He turned away, and emptying all his eggs into the hat of a little urchin who stood near, walked out of the churchyard. He did not stop to exchange another word with any one; neither with the men who stood all *endimanchés* before the stores, nor the women who were mounting upon horses and into vehicles, or walking in groups to their homes.

He took a short cut across the cotton-field that extended back of the town, and walking rapidly, soon reached his home. It was a pleasant house of few rooms and many windows, with fresh air blowing through from every side; his workshop was beside it. A broad strip of greensward, studded here and there with trees, sloped down to the road.

Azenor entered the kitchen, where an amiable old black woman was chopping onion and sage at a table.

"Tranquiline," he said abruptly, "they's a young girl goin' to pass yere afta a w'ile. She's got a blue dress an' w'ite josie on, an' a veil on her head. W'en you see her, I want you to go to the road an' make her res' there on the bench, an' ask her if she don't want a cup o' coffee. I saw her go to communion, me; so she did n't eat any break-fas'. Eve'ybody else f'om out o' town, that went to communion, got invited somew'ere another. It's enough to make a person sick to see such meanness."

"An' you want me ter go down to de gate, jis' so, an' ax 'er pineblank ef she wants some coffee?" asked the bewildered Tranquiline.

"I don't care if you ask her poin' blank o' not; but you do like I say." Tranquiline was leaning over the gate when Lalie came along.

"Howdy," offered the woman.

"Howdy," the girl returned.

"Did you see a yalla calf wid black spots a t'arm' down de lane, missy?"

"Non; not yalla, an' not with black spot'. *Mais* I see one li'le w'ite calf tie by a rope, yonda 'roun' the ben'."

"Dat warn't hit. Dis heah one was yalla. I hope he done flung hisse'f down de bank an' broke his nake. Sarve 'im right! But whar you come f'om, chile? You look plum wo' out. Set down dah on dat bench, an' le' me fotch you a cup o' coffee."

Azenor had already in his eagerness arranged a tray, upon which was a smoking cup of *café au lait*. He had buttered and jellied generous slices of bread, and was searching wildly for something when Tranquiline reëntered.

"W'at become o' that half of chicken-pie, Tranquiline, that was yere in the *garde manger* yesterday?"

"W'at chicken-pie? W'at *garde manger*?" blustered the woman.

"Like we got mo' 'en one *garde manger* in the house, Tranquiline!"

"You jis' like ole Ma'ame Azenor use' to be, you is! You 'spec' chicken-pie gwine las' etarnal? W'en some'pin done sp'ilt, I flings it' way. Dat's me—dat's Tranquiline!"

So Azenor resigned himself,—what else could he do?—and sent the tray, incomplete, as he fancied it, out to Lalie.

He trembled at thought of what he did; he, whose nerves were usually as steady as some piece of steel mechanism.

Would it anger her if she suspected? Would it please her if she knew? Would she say this or that to Tranquiline? And would Tranquiline tell him truly what she said—how she looked?

As it was Sunday, Azenor did not work that afternoon. Instead, he took a book out under the trees, as he often did, and sat reading it, from the first sound of the Vesper bell, that came faintly across the fields, till the Angelus. All that time! He turned many a page, yet in the end did not know what he had read. With his pencil he had traced "Lalie" upon every margin, and was saying it softly to himself.

Another Sunday Azenor saw Lalie at mass—and again. Once he walked with her and showed her the short cut across the cotton-field. She was very glad that day, and told him she was going to work—her grandmother said she might. She was going to hoe, up in the fields with Monsieur Le Blôt's hands. He entreated her not to; and when she asked his reason, he could not tell her, but turned and tore shyly and savagely at the elder-blossoms that grew along the fence.

Then they stopped where she was going to cross the fence from the field into the lane. He wanted to tell her that was his house which they could see not far away; but he did not dare to, since he had fed her there on the morning she was hungry.

"An' you say yo' gran'ma's goin' to let you work? She keeps you f'om workin', *donc*?" He wanted to question her about her grandmother, and could think of no other way to begin.

"Po' ole grand'mère!" she answered. "I don' b'lieve she know mos' time w'at she's doin'. Sometime she say' I aint no betta an' one nigga, an' she fo'ce me to work. Then she say she know I'm goin' be one canaille like maman, an' she make me set down still, like she would want to kill me if I would move. Her, she on'y want' to be out in the wood', day an' night, day an' night. She ain' got her right head, po' grand'mère. I know she ain't."

Lalie had spoken low and in jerks, as if every word gave her pain. Azenor could feel her distress as plainly as he saw it. He wanted to say something to her—to do something for her. But her mere presence paralyzed him into inactivity—except his pulses, that beat like hammers when he was with her. Such a poor, shabby little thing as she was, too!

"I'm goin' to wait yere nex' Sunday fo' you, Lalie," he said, when the fence was between them. And he thought he had said something very daring.

But the next Sunday she did not come. She was neither at the appointed place of meeting in the lane, nor was she at mass. Her absence—so unexpected—affected Azenor like a calamity. Late in the afternoon, when he could stand the trouble and bewilderment of it no longer, he went and leaned over Père Antoine's fence. The priest was picking the slugs from his roses on the other side.

"That young girl from the Bon-Dieu," said Azenor—"she was not at mass to-day. I suppose her grandmother has forgotten your warning."

"No," answered the priest. "The child is ill, I hear. Butrand tells me she has been ill for several days from overwork in the fields. I shall go out to-morrow to see about her. I would go to-day, if I could."

"The child is ill," was all Azenor heard or understood of Père Antoine's words. He turned and walked resolutely away, like one who determines suddenly upon action after meaningless hesitation.

He walked towards his home and past it, as if it were a spot that did not concern him. He went on down the lane and into the wood where he had seen Lalie disappear that day.

Here all was shadow, for the sun had dipped too low in the west to send a single ray through the dense foliage of the forest.

Now that he found himself on the way to Lalie's home, he strove to understand why he had not gone there before. He often visited other girls in the village and neighborhood,—why not have gone to her, as well? The answer lay too deep in his heart for him to be more than half-conscious of it. Fear had kept him,—dread to see her desolate life face to face. He did not know how he could bear it.

But now he was going to her at last. She was ill. He would stand upon that dismantled porch that he could just remember. Doubtless Ma'ame Zidore would come out to know his will, and he would tell her that Père Antoine had sent to inquire how Mamzelle Lalie was. No! Why drag in Père Antoine? He would simply stand boldly and say, "Ma'ame Zidore, I learn that Lalie is ill. I have come to know if it is true, and to see her, if I may."

When Azenor reached the cabin where Lalie dwelt, all sign of day had vanished. Dusk had fallen swiftly after the sunset. The moss that hung heavy from great live-oak branches was making fantastic silhouettes against the eastern sky that the big, round moon was beginning to light. Off in the swamp beyond the bayou, hundreds of dismal voices were droning a lullaby. Upon the hovel itself, a stillness like death rested.

Oftener than once Azenor tapped upon the door, which was closed as well as it could be, without obtaining a reply. He finally approached one of the small unglazed windows, in which coarse mosquito-netting had been fastened, and looked into the room.

By the moonlight slanting in he could see Lalie stretched upon a bed; but of Ma'ame Zidore there was no sign. "Lalie!" he called softly. "Lalie!"

The girl slightly moved her head upon the pillow. Then he boldly opened the door and entered.

Upon a wretched bed, over which was spread a cover of patched calico, Lalie lay, her frail body only half concealed by the single garment that was upon it. One hand was plunged beneath her pillow; the other, which was free, he touched. It was as hot as flame; so was her head. He knelt sobbing upon the floor beside her, and called her his love and his soul. He begged her to speak a word to him,—to look at him. But she only muttered disjointedly that the cotton was all turning to ashes in the fields, and the blades of the corn were in flames.

If he was choked with love and grief to see her so, he was moved by anger as well; rage against himself, against Père Antoine, against the people upon the plantation and in the village, who had so abandoned a helpless creature to misery and maybe death. Because she had been silent—had not lifted her voice in complaint—they believed she suffered no more than she could bear.

But surely the people could not be utterly without heart. There must be one somewhere with the spirit of Christ. Père Antoine would tell him of such a one, and he would carry Lalie to her,—out of this atmosphere of death. He was in haste to be gone with her. He fancied every moment of delay was a fresh danger threatening her life.

He folded the rude bed-cover over Lalie's naked limbs, and lifted her in his arms. She made no resistance. She seemed only loath to withdraw her hand from beneath the pillow. When she did, he saw that she held lightly but firmly clasped in her encircling fingers the pretty Easter-egg he had given her! He uttered a low cry of exultation as the full significance of this came over him. If she had hung for hours upon his neck telling him that she loved him, he could not have known it more surely than by this sign. Azenor felt as if some mysterious bond had all at once drawn them heart to heart and made them one.

No need now to go from door to door begging admittance for her. She was his. She belonged to him. He knew now where her place was, whose roof must shelter her, and whose arms protect her.

So Azenor, with his loved one in his arms, walked through the forest, sure-footed as a panther. Once, as he walked, he could hear in the distance the weird chant which Ma'ame Zidore was crooning—to the moon, maybe—as she gathered her wood.

Once, where the water was trickling cool through rocks, he stopped to lave Lalie's hot cheeks and hands and forehead. He had not once touched his lips to her. But now, when a sudden great fear came upon him because she did not know him, instinctively he pressed his lips upon hers that were parched and burning. He held them there till hers were soft and pliant from the healthy moisture of his own.

Then she knew him. She did not tell him so, but her stiffened fingers relaxed their tense hold upon the Easter bauble. It fell to the ground as she twined her arm around his neck; and he understood.

"Stay close by her, Tranquiline," said Azenor, when he had laid Lalie upon his own couch at home. "I'm goin' for the doctor en' for Père Antoine. Not because she is goin' to die," he added hastily, seeing the awe that crept into the woman's face at mention of the priest. "She is goin' to live! Do you think I would let my wife die, Tranquiline?"

Loka

She was a half-breed Indian girl, with hardly a rag to her back. To the ladies of the Band of United Endeavor who questioned her, she said her name was Loka, and she did not know where she belonged, unless it was on Bayou Choctaw.

She had appeared one day at the side door of Frobissaint's "oyster saloon" in Natchitoches, asking for food. Frobissaint, a practical philanthropist, engaged her on the spot as tumbler-washer.

She was not successful at that; she broke too many tumblers. But, as Frobissaint charged her with the broken glasses, he did not mind, until she began to break them over the heads of his customers. Then he seized her by the wrist and dragged her before the Band of United Endeavor, then in session around the corner. This was considerate on Frobissaint's part, for he could have dragged her just as well to the police station.

Loka was not beautiful, as she stood in her red calico rags before the scrutinizing band. Her coarse, black, unkempt hair framed a broad, swarthy face without a redeeming feature, except eyes that were not bad; slow in their movements, but frank eyes enough. She was big—boned and clumsy.

She did not know how old she was. The minister's wife reckoned she might be sixteen. The judge's wife thought that it made no difference. The doctor's wife suggested that the girl have a bath and change before she be handled, even in discussion. The motion was not seconded. Loka's ultimate disposal was an urgent and difficult consideration.

Some one mentioned a reformatory. Every one else objected.

Madame Laballière, the planter's wife, knew a respectable family of 'Cadians living some miles below, who, she thought, would give the girl a home, with benefit to all concerned. The 'Cadian woman was a deserving one, with a large family of small children, who had all her own work to do. The husband cropped in a modest way. Loka would not only be taught to work at the Padues', but would receive a good moral training beside.

That settled it. Every one agreed with the planter's wife that it was a chance in a thousand;-and Loka was sent to sit on the steps outside, while the band proceeded to the business next in order.

Loka was afraid of treading upon the little Padues when she first got amongst them,—there were so many of them,—and her feet were like leaden weights, encased in the strong brogans with which the band had equipped her.

Madame Padue, a small, black-eyed, aggressive woman, questioned her in a sharp, direct fashion peculiar to herself.

"How come you don't talk French, you?" Loka shrugged her shoulders.

"I kin talk English good 's anybody; an' lit' bit Choctaw, too," she offered, apologetically.

"*Ma foi*, you kin fo'git yo' Choctaw. Soona the betta for me. Now if you wil-lin', an' ent too lazy an' sassy, we 'll git 'long somehow. *Vrai sauvage ça*," she muttered under her breath, as she turned to initiate Loka into some of her new duties.

She herself was a worker. A good deal more fussy one than her easy-going husband and children thought necessary or agreeable. Loka's slow ways and heavy motions aggravated her. It was in vain Monsieur Padue expostulated:—

"She's on'y a chile, rememba, Tontine."

"She's *vrai sauvage*, that's w'at. It's got to be work out of her," was Tontine's only reply to such remonstrance.

The girl was indeed so deliberate about her tasks that she had to be urged constantly to accomplish the amount of labor that Tontine required of her. Moreover, she carried to her work a stolid indifference that was exasperating. Whether at the wash-tub, scrubbing the floors, weeding the garden, or learning her lessons and catechism with the children on Sundays, it was the same.

It was only when intrusted with the care of little Bibine, the baby, that Loka crept somewhat out of her apathy. She grew very fond of him. No wonder; such a baby as he was! So good, so fat, and complaisant! He had such, a way of clasping Loka's broad face between his pudgy fists and savagely biting her chin with his hard, toothless gums! Such a way of bouncing in her arms as if he were mounted upon springs! At his antics the girl would laugh a wholesome, ringing laugh that was good to hear.

She was left alone to watch and nurse him one day. An accommodating neighbor who had become the possessor of a fine new spring wagon passed by just after the noon-hour meal, and offered to take the whole family on a jaunt to town. The offer was all the more tempting as Tontine had some long-delayed shopping to do; and the opportunity to equip the children with shoes and summer hats could not be slighted. So away they all went. All but Bibine, who was left swinging in his branle with only Loka for company.

This branle consisted of a strong circular piece of cotton cloth, securely but slackly fastened to a large, stout hoop suspended by three light cords to a hook in a rafter of the gallery. The baby who has not swung in a branle does not know the quintessence of baby luxury. In each of the four rooms of the house was a hook from which to hang this swing.

Often it was taken out under the trees. But to-day it swung in the shade of the open gallery; and Loka sat beside it, giving it now and then a slight impetus that sent it circling in slow, sleep-inspiring undulations.

Bibine kicked and cooed as long as he was able. But Loka was humming a monotonous lullaby; the branle was swaying to and fro, the warm air fanning him deliciously; and Bibine was soon fast asleep.

Seeing this, Loka quietly let down the mosquito net, to protect the child's slumber from the intrusion of the many insects that were swarming in the summer air.

Singularly enough, there was no work for her to do; and Tontine, in her hurried departure, had failed to provide for the emergency. The washing and ironing were over; the floors had been scrubbed, and the rooms righted; the yard swept; the chickens fed; vegetables picked and washed. There was absolutely nothing to do, and Loka gave herself up to the dreams of idleness.

As she sat comfortably back in the roomy rocker, she let her eyes sweep lazily across the country. Away off to the right peeped up, from amid densely clustered trees, the pointed roofs and long pipe of the steam-gin of Laballière's. No other habitation was visible except a few low, flat dwellings far over the river, that could hardly be seen.

The immense plantation took up all the land in sight. The few acres that Baptiste Padue cultivated were his own, that Laballière, out of friendly consideration, had sold to him. Baptiste's fine crop of cotton and corn was "laid by" just now, waiting for rain; and Baptiste had gone with the rest of the family to town. Beyond the river and the field and everywhere about were dense woods.

Loka's gaze, that had been slowly traveling along the edge of the horizon, finally fastened upon the woods, and stayed there. Into her eyes came the absent look of one whose thought is projected into the future or the past, leaving the present blank. She was seeing a vision. It had come with a whiff that the strong south breeze had blown to her from the woods.

She was seeing old Marot, the squaw who drank whiskey and plaited baskets and beat her. There was something, after all, in being beaten, if only to scream out and fight back, as at that time in Natchitoches, when she broke a glass on the head of a man who laughed at her and pulled her hair, and called her "fool names."

Old Marot wanted her to steal and cheat, to beg and lie, when they went out with the baskets to sell. Loka did not want to. She did not like to. That was why she had run away—and because she was beaten. But—but ah! the scent of the sassafras leaves hanging to dry in the shade! The pungent, camomile! The sound of the bayou tumbling over that old slimy log! Only to lie there for hours and watch the glistening lizards glide in and out was worth a beating.

She knew the birds must be singing in chorus out there in the woods where the gray moss was hanging, and the trumpet-vine trailing from the trees, spangled with blossoms. In spirit she heard the songsters.

She wondered if Choctaw Joe and Sambite played dice every night by the camp-fire as they used to do; and if they still fought and slashed each other when wild with drink. How good it felt to walk with moccasined feet over the springy turf, under the trees! What fun to trap the squirrels, to skin the otter; to take those swift flights on the pony that Choctaw Joe had stolen from the Texans!

Loka sat motionless; only her breast heaved tumultuously. Her heart was aching with savage homesickness. She could not feel just then that the sin and pain of that life were anything beside the joy of its freedom.

Loka was sick for the woods. She felt she must die if she could not get back to them, and to her vagabond life. Was there anything to hinder her? She stooped and unlaced the brogans that were chafing her feet, removed them and her stockings, and threw the things away from her. She stood up all a-quiver, panting, ready for flight.

But there was a sound that stopped her. It was little Bibine, cooing, sputtering, battling hands and feet with the mosquito net that he had dragged over his face. The girl uttered a sob as she reached down for the baby she had grown to love so, and clasped him in her arms. She could not go and leave Bibine behind.

TONTINE BEGAN TO GRUMBLE AT once when she discovered that Loka was not at hand to receive them on their return.

"*Bon!*" she exclaimed. "Now w'ere is that Loka? Ah, that girl, she aggravates me too much. Firs' thing she knows I'm goin' sen' her straight back to them ban' of lady w'ere she come frum."

"Loka!" she called, in short, sharp tones, as she traversed the house and peered into each room. "Lo—ka!" She cried loudly enough to be heard half a mile away when she got out upon the back gallery. Again and again she called.

Baptiste was exchanging the discomfort of his Sunday coat for the accustomed ease of shirt sleeves.

"*Mais* don't git so excite, Tontine," he implored. "I'm sho she's yonda to the crib shellin' co'n, or somew'ere like that."

"Run, François, you, an' see to the crib," the mother commanded. "Bibine mus' be starve! Run to the hen-house an' look, Juliette. Maybe she's fall asleep in some corna. That 'll learn me 'notha time to go trus' *une pareille sauvage* with my baby, *va!*"

When it was discovered that Loka was nowhere in the immediate vicinity, Tontine was furious.

"*Pas possible* she's walk to Laballière, with Bibine!" she exclaimed.

"I'll saddle the hoss an' go see, Tontine," interposed Baptiste, who was beginning to share his wife's uneasiness.

"Go, go, Baptiste," she urged. "An' you, boys, run yonda down the road to ole Aunt Judy's cabin an' see."

It was found that Loka had not been seen at Laballière's, nor at Aunt Judy's cabin; that she had not taken the boat, that was still fastened to its moorings down the bank. Then Tontine's excitement left her. She turned pale and sat quietly down in her room, with an unnatural calm that frightened the children.

Some of them began to cry. Baptiste walked restlessly about, anxiously scanning the country in all directions. A wretched hour dragged by. The sun had set, leaving hardly an afterglow, and in a little while the twilight that falls so swiftly would be there.

Baptiste was preparing to mount his horse, to start out again on the round he had already been over. Tontine sat in the same state of intense abstraction when Francois, who had perched himself among the lofty branches of a chinaberry-tree, called out: "Ent that Loka 'way yon'a, jis' come out de wood? climbin' de fence down by de melon patch?"

It was difficult to distinguish in the gathering dusk if the figure were that of man or beast. But the family was not left long in suspense. Baptiste sped his horse away in the direction indicated by Francis, and in a little while he was galloping back with Bibine in his arms; as fretful, sleepy and hungry a baby as ever was.

Loka came trudging on behind Baptiste. He did not wait for explanations; he was too eager to place the child in the arms of its mother. The suspense over, Tontine began to cry; that followed naturally, of course. Through her tears she managed to address Loka, who stood all tattered and disheveled in the doorway: "W'ere you been? Tell me that."

"Bibine an' me," answered Loka, slowly and awkwardly, "we was lonesome—we been take lit' 'broad in de wood."

"You did n' know no betta 'an to take 'way Bibine like that? W'at Ma'ame Laballière mean, anyhow, to sen' me such a objec' like you, I want to know?"

"You go'n' sen' me 'way?" asked Loka, passing her hand in a hopeless fashion over her frowzy hair.

"*Par exemple!* straight you march back to that ban' w'ere you come from. To give me such a fright like that! *pas possible*."

"Go slow, Tontine; go slow," interposed Baptiste.

"Don' sen' me 'way frum Bibine," entreated the girl, with a note in her voice like a lament.

"To-day," she went on, in her dragging manner, "I want to run 'way bad, an' take to de wood; an' go yonda back to Bayou Choctaw to steal an' lie agin. It's on'y Bibine w'at hole me back. I could n' lef' 'im. I could n' do dat. An' we jis' go take lit' 'broad in de wood, das all, him an' me. Don' sen' me 'way like dat!"

Baptiste led the girl gently away to the far end of the gallery, and spoke soothingly to her. He told her to be good and brave, and he would right the trouble for her. He left her standing there and went back to his wife.

"Tontine," he began, with unusual energy, "you got to listen to the truth—once fo' all." He had evidently determined to profit by his wife's lachrymose and wilted condition to assert his authority.

"I want to say who's masta in this house—it's me," he went on. Tontine did not protest; only clasped the baby a little closer, which encouraged him to proceed.

"You been grind that girl too much. She ent a bad girl—I been watch her close, 'count of the chil'ren; she ent bad. All she want, it's li'le mo' rope. You can't drive a ox with the same gearin' you drive a mule. You got to learn that, Tontine."

He approached his wife's chair and stood beside her.

"That girl, she done tole us how she was temp' to-day to turn *canaille*—like we all temp' sometime'. W'at was it save her? That li'le chile w'at you hole in yo' arm. An' now you want to take her guarjun angel 'way f'om her? *Non, non, ma femme*," he said, resting his hand gently upon his wife's head. "We got to rememba she ent like you an' me, po' thing; she's one Injun, her."

BOULÔT AND BOULOTTE

When Boulôt and Boulotte, the little piny-wood twins, had reached the dignified age of twelve, it was decided in family council that the time had come for them to put their little naked feet into shoes. They were two brown-skinned, black-eyed 'Cadian roly-polies, who lived with father and mother and a troop of brothers and sisters halfway up the hill, in a neat log cabin that had a substantial mud chimney at one end. They could well afford shoes now, for they had saved many a picayune through their industry of selling wild grapes, blackberries, and "socoes" to ladies in the village who "put up" such things.

Boulôt and Boulotte were to buy the shoes themselves, and they selected a Saturday afternoon for the important transaction, for that is the great shopping time in Natchitoches Parish. So upon a bright Saturday afternoon Boulôt and Boulotte, hand in hand, with their quarters, their dimes, and their picayunes tied carefully in a Sunday handkerchief, descended the hill, and disappeared from the gaze of the eager group that had assembled to see them go.

Long before it was time for their return, this same small band, with ten year old Seraphine at their head, holding a tiny Seraphin in her arms, had stationed themselves in a row before the cabin at a convenient point from which to make quick and careful observation.

Even before the two could be caught sight of, their chattering voices were heard down by the spring, where they had doubtless stopped to drink. The voices grew more and more audible. Then, through the branches of the young pines, Boulotte's blue sun-bonnet appeared, and Boulôt's straw hat. Finally the twins, hand in hand, stepped into the clearing in full view.

Consternation seized the band.

"You bof crazy *donc*, Boulôt an' Boulotte," screamed Seraphine. "You go buy shoes, an' come home barefeet like you was go!"

Boulôt flushed crimson. He silently hung his head, and looked sheepishly down at his bare feet, then at the fine stout brogans that he carried in his hand. He had not thought of it.

Boulotte also carried shoes, but of the glossiest, with the highest of heels and brightest of buttons. But she was not one to be disconcerted or to look sheepish; far from it.

"You 'spec' Boulôt an' me we got money fur was'e—us?" she retorted, with withering condescension. "You think we go buy shoes fur ruin it in de dus'? *Comment!*"

And they all walked into the house crest-fallen; all but Boulotte, who was mistress of the situation, and Seraphin, who did not care one way or the other.

FOR MARSE CHOUCHOUTE

A n' now, young man, w'at you want to remember is this—an' take it fer yo' motto: 'No monkey-shines with Uncle Sam.' You undastan'? You aware now o' the penalties attached to monkey-shinin' with Uncle Sam. I reckon that's 'bout all I got to say; so you be on han' promp' to-morrow mornin' at seven o'clock, to take charge o' the United States mail-bag."

This formed the close of a very pompous address delivered by the postmaster of Cloutier ville to young Armand Verchette, who had been appointed to carry the mails from the village to the railway station three miles away.

Armand—or Chouchoute, as every one chose to call him, following the habit of the Creoles in giving nicknames—had heard the man a little impatiently.

Not so the negro boy who accompanied him. The child had listened with the deepest respect and awe to every word of the rambling admonition.

"How much you gwine git, Marse Chouchoute?" he asked, as they walked down the village street together, the black boy a little behind. He was very black, and slightly deformed; a small boy, scarcely reaching to the shoulder of his companion, whose cast-off garments he wore. But Chouchoute was tall for his sixteen years, and carried himself well.

"W'y, I'm goin' to git thirty dolla' a month, Wash; w'at you say to that? Betta 'an hoein' cotton, ain't it?" He laughed with a triumphant ring in his voice.

But Wash did not laugh; he was too much impressed by the importance of this new function, too much bewildered by the vision of sudden wealth which thirty dollars a month meant to his understanding.

He felt, too, deeply conscious of the great weight of responsibility which this new office brought with it. The imposing salary had confirmed the impression left by the postmaster's words.

"*You* gwine git all dat money? Sakes! W'at you reckon Ma'ame Verchette say? I know she gwine mos' take a fit w'en she heah dat."

But Chouchoute's mother did not "mos' take a fit" when she heard of her son's good fortune. The white and wasted hand which she rested upon the boy's black curls trembled a little, it is true, and tears of emotion came into her tired eyes. This step seemed to her the beginning of better things for her fatherless boy.

They lived quite at the end of this little French village, which was simply two long rows of very old frame houses, facing each other closely across a dusty roadway.

Their home was a cottage, so small and so humble that it just escaped the reproach of being a cabin.

Every one was kind to Madame Verchette. Neighbors ran in of mornings to help her with her work—she could do so little for herself. And often the good priest, Père Antoine, came to sit with her and talk innocent gossip.

To say that Wash was fond of Madame Verchette and her son is to be poor in language to express devotion. He worshiped her as if she were already an angel in Paradise.

Chouchoute was a delightful young fellow; no one could help loving him. His heart was as warm and cheery as his own southern sunbeams. If he was born with an unlucky trick of forgetfulness—or better, thoughtlessness—no one ever felt much like blaming him for it, so much did it seem a part of his happy, careless nature. And why was that faithful watch-dog, Wash, always at Marse Chouchoute's heels, if it were not to be hands and ears and eyes to him, more than half the time?

One beautiful spring night, Chouchoute, on his way to the station, was riding along the road that skirted the river. The clumsy mail-bag that lay before him across the pony was almost empty; for the Cloutierville mail was a meagre and unimportant one at best.

But he did not know this. He was not thinking of the mail, in fact; he was only feeling that life was very agreeable this delicious spring night.

There were cabins at intervals upon the road—most of them darkened, for the hour was late. As he approached one of these, which was more pretentious than the others, he heard the sound of a fiddle, and saw lights through the openings of the house.

It was so far from the road that when he stopped his horse and peered through the darkness he could not recognize the dancers who passed before the open doors and windows. But he knew this was Gros-Léon's ball, which he had heard the boys talking about all the week.

Why should he not go and stand in the doorway an instant and exchange a word with the dancers?

Chouchoute dismounted, fastened his horse to the fence-post, and proceeded towards the house.

The room, crowded with people young and old, was long and low, with rough beams across the ceiling, blackened by smoke and time. Upon the high mantelpiece a single coal-oil lamp burned, and none too brightly.

In a far corner, upon a platform of boards laid across two flour barrels, sat Uncle Ben, playing upon a squeaky fiddle, and shouting the "figures."

"Ah! *v'là* Chouchoute!" some one called.

"Eh! Chouchoute!"

"Jus' in time, Chouchoute; yere's Miss Léontine waitin' fer a partna."

"S'lute yo' partnas!" Uncle Ben was thundering forth; and Chouchoute, with one hand gracefully behind him, made a profound bow to Miss Léontine, as he offered her the other.

Now Chouchoute was noted far and wide for his skill as a dancer. The moment he stood upon the floor, a fresh spirit seemed to enter into all present. It was with renewed vigor that Uncle Ben intoned his "Balancy all! Fus' fo' fo'ard an' back!"

The spectators drew close about the couples to watch Chouchoute's wonderful performance; his pointing of toes; his pigeonwings in which his feet seemed hardly to touch the floor.

"It take Chouchoute to show 'em de step, *va!*" proclaimed Gros-Léon, with a fat satisfaction, to the audience at large.

"Look 'im; look 'im yonda! Ole Ben got to work hard' 'an dat, if he want to keep up wid Chouchoute, I tell you!".

So it was; encouragement and adulation on all sides, till, from the praise that was showered on him, Chouchoute's head was soon as light as his feet.

At the windows appeared the dusky faces of negroes, their bright eyes gleaming as they viewed the scene within and mingled their loud guffaws with the medley of sound that was already deafening.

The time was speeding. The air was heavy in the room, but no one seemed to mind this. Uncle Ben was calling the figures now with a rhythmic sing-song:—

"Right an' lef' all 'roun'! Swing co'nas!"

Chouchoute turned with a smile to Miss Félicie on his left, his hand extended, when what should break upon his ear but the long, harrowing wail of a locomotive!

Before the sound ceased he had vanished from the room. Miss

Félicie stood as he left her, with hand uplifted, rooted to the spot with astonishment.

It was the train whistling for his station, and he a mile and more away! He knew he was too late, and that he could not make the distance; but the sound had been a rude reminder that he was not at his post of duty.

However, he would do what he could now. He ran swiftly to the outer road, and to the spot where he had left his pony.

The horse was gone, and with it the United States mail-bag!

For an instant Chouchoute stood half-stunned with terror. Then, in one quick flash, came to his mind a vision of possibilities that sickened him. Disgrace overtaking him in this position of trust; poverty his portion again; and his dear mother forced to share both with him.

He turned desperately to some negroes who had followed him, seeing his wild rush from the house:—

"Who saw my hoss? W'at you all did with my hoss, say?"

"Who you reckon tech yo' hoss, boy?" grumbled Gustave, a sullen-looking mulatto. "You did n'have no call to lef''im in de road, fus' place."

"'Pear to me like I heahed a hoss a-lopin' down de road jis' now; did n' you, Uncle Jake?" ventured a second.

"Neva heahed nuttin'—nuttin' 't all, 'cep' dat big-mouf Ben yon da makin' mo' fuss 'an a t'unda-sto'm."

"Boys!" cried Chouchoute, excitedly, "bring me a hoss, quick, one of you. I'm boun' to have one! I'm boun' to! I 'll give two dolla' to the firs' man brings me a hoss."

Near at hand, in the "lot" that adjoined Uncle Jake's cabin, was his little creole pony, nibbling the cool, wet grass that he found, along the edges and in the corners of the fence.

The negro led the pony forth. With no further word, and with one bound, Chouchoute was upon the animal's back. He wanted neither saddle nor bridle, for there were few horses in the neighborhood that had not been trained to be guided by the simple motions of a rider's body.

Once mounted, he threw himself forward with a certain violent impulse, leaning till his cheek touched the animal's mane.

He uttered a sharp "Hei!" and at once, as if possessed by sudden frenzy, the horse dashed forward, leaving the bewildered black men in a cloud of dust.

What a mad ride it was! On one side was the river bank, steep in places and crumbling away; on the other, an unbroken line of fencing;

now in straight lines of neat planking, now treacherous barbed wire, sometimes the zigzag rail.

The night was black, with only such faint light as the stars were shedding. No sound was to be heard save the quick thud of the horse's hoofs upon the hard dirt road, the animal's heavy breathing, and the boy's feverish "hei-hei!" when he fancied the speed slackened.

Occasionally a marauding dog started from the obscurity to bark and give useless chase.

"To the road, to the road, Bon-à-rien!" panted Chouchoute, for the horse in his wild race had approached so closely to the river's edge that the bank crumbled beneath his flying feet. It was only by a desperate lunge and bound that he saved himself and rider from plunging into the water below.

Chouchoute hardly knew what he was pursuing so madly. It was rather something that drove him; fear, hope, desperation.

He was rushing to the station, because it seemed to him, naturally, the first thing to do. There was the faint hope that his own horse had broken rein and gone there of his own accord; but such hope was almost lost in a wretched conviction that had seized him the instant he saw "Gustave the thief" among the men gathered at Gros-Léon's. "Hei! hei, Bon-à-rien!"

The lights of the railway station were gleaming ahead, and Chouchoute's hot ride was almost at an end.

With sudden and strange perversity of purpose, Chouchoute, as he drew closer upon the station, slackened his horse's speed. A low fence was in his way. Not long before, he would have cleared it at a bound, for Bon-à-rien could do such things. Now he cantered easily to the end of it, to go through the gate which was there.

His courage was growing faint, and his heart sinking within him as he drew nearer and nearer.

He dismounted, and holding the pony by the mane, approached with some trepidation the young station-master, who was taking note of some freight that had been deposited near the tracks.

"Mr. Hudson," faltered Chouchoute, "did you see my pony 'roun' yere anywhere? an'—an' the mail-sack?"

"Your pony's safe in the woods, Chou'te. The mail-bag's on its way to New Orleans"—

"Thank God!" breathed the boy.

"But that poor little fool darkey of yours has about done it for himself, I guess."

"Wash? Oh, Mr. Hudson! w'at's—w'at's happen' to Wash?"

"He's inside there, on my mattress. He's hurt, and he's hurt bad; that's what's the matter. You see the ten forty-five had come in, and she did n't make much of a stop; she was just pushing out, when bless me if that little chap of yours didn't come tearing along on Spunky as if Old Harry was behind him.

"You know how No. 22 can pull at the start; and there was that little imp keeping abreast of her 'most under the thing's wheels.

"I shouted at him. I could n't make out what he was up to, when blamed if he did n't pitch the mail-bag clean into the car! Buffalo Bill could n't have done it neater.

"Then Spunky, she shied; and Wash he bounced against the side of that car and back, like a rubber ball, and laid in the ditch till we carried him inside.

"I've wired down the road for Doctor Campbell to come up on 14 and do what he can for him."

Hudson had related these events to the distracted boy while they made their way toward the house.

Inside, upon a low pallet, lay the little negro, breathing heavily, his black face pinched and ashen with approaching death. He had wanted no one to touch him further than to lay him upon the bed.

The few men and colored women gathered in the room were looking upon him with pity mingled with curiosity.

When he saw Chouchoute he closed his eyes, and a shiver passed through his small frame. Those about him thought he was dead. Chouchoute knelt, choking, at his side and held his hand.

"O Wash, Wash! W'at you did that for? W'at made you, Wash?"

"Marse Chouchoute," the boy whispered, so low that no one could hear him but his friend, "I was gwine 'long de big road, pas' Marse Gros-Léon's, an' I seed Spunky tied dah wid de mail. Dar warn't a minute—I 'clar', Marse Chouchoute, dar warn't a minute—to fotch you. W'at makes my head tu'n 'roun' dat away?"

"Neva mine, Wash; keep still; don't you try to talk," entreated Chouchoute.

"You ain't mad, Marse Chouchoute?"

The lad could only answer with a hand pressure.

"Dar warn't a minute, so I gits top o' Spunky—I neva seed nuttin' d'ar de road like dat. I come 'long side—de train—an' fling de sack. I seed 'im kotch it, and I don' know nuttin' mo' 'cep' mis'ry, tell I see you—a-comin' frough de do'. Mebby Ma'ame Armand know some'pin," he murmured faintly, "w'at gwine make my—head quit tu'nin' 'round dat away. I boun' to git well, 'ca'se who—gwine—watch Marse—Chouchoute?"

A Visit to Avoyelles

Every one who came up from Avoyelles had the same story to tell of Mentine. *Cher Maître!* but she was changed. And there were babies, more than she could well manage; as good as four already. Jules was not kind except to himself. They seldom went to church, and never anywhere upon a visit. They lived as poorly as pine-woods people. Doudouce had heard the story often, the last time no later than that morning.

"Ho-a!" he shouted to his mule plumb in the middle of the cotton row. He had staggered along behind the plow since early morning, and of a sudden he felt he had had enough of it. He mounted the mule and rode away to the stable, leaving the plow with its polished blade thrust deep in the red Cane River soil. His head felt like a windmill with the recollections and sudden intentions that had crowded it and were whirling through his brain since he had heard the last story about Mentine.

He knew well enough Mentine would have married him seven years ago had not Jules Trodon come up from Avoyelles and captivated her with his handsome eyes and pleasant speech. Doudouce was resigned then, for he held Mentine's happiness above his own. But now she was suffering in a hopeless, common, exasperating way for the small comforts of life. People had told him so. And somehow, to-day, he could not stand the knowledge passively. He felt he must see those things they spoke of with his own eyes. He must strive to help her and her children if it were possible.

Doudouce could not sleep that night. He lay with wakeful eyes watching the moonlight creep across the bare floor of his room; listening to sounds that seemed unfamiliar and weird down among the rushes along the bayou. But towards morning he saw Mentine as he had seen her last in her white wedding gown and veil. She looked at him with appealing eyes and held out her arms for protection,—for, rescue, it seemed to him. That dream determined him. The following day Doudouce started for Avoyelles.

Jules Trodon's home lay a mile or two from Marksville. It consisted of three rooms strung in a row and opening upon a narrow gallery. The whole wore an aspect of poverty and dilapidation that summer day, towards noon, when Doudouce approached it. His presence outside the gate aroused the frantic barking of dogs that dashed down the steps as if to attack him. Two little brown barefooted children, a boy and girl, stood upon the gallery staring stupidly at him. "Call off you' dogs," he requested; but they only continued to stare.

"Down, Pluto! down, Achille!" cried the shrill voice of a woman who emerged from the house, holding upon her arm a delicate baby of a year or two. There was only an instant of unrecognition.

"*Mais* Doudouce, that ent you, *comment!* Well, if any one would tole me this mornin'! Git a chair, 'Tit Jules. That's Mista Doudouce, f'om 'way yonda Natchitoches w'ere yo' maman use' to live. *Mais*, you ent change'; you' lookin' well, Doudouce."

He shook hands in a slow, undemonstrative way, and seated himself clumsily upon the hide-bottomed chair, laying his broad-rimmed felt hat upon the floor beside him. He was very uncomfortable in the cloth Sunday coat which he wore.

"I had business that call' me to Marksville," he began, "an' I say to myse'f, *'Tiens*, you can't pass by without tell' 'em all howdy.'"

"*Par exemple!* w'at Jules would said to that! *Mais*, you' lookin' well; you ent change', Doudouce."

"An' you' lookin' well, Mentine, Jis' the same Mentine." He regretted that he lacked talent to make the lie bolder.

She moved a little uneasily, and felt upon her shoulder for a pin with which to fasten the front of her old gown where it lacked a button. She had kept the baby in her lap. Doudouce was wondering miserably if he would have known her outside her home. He would have known her sweet, cheerful brown eyes, that were not changed; but her figure, that had looked so trim in the wedding gown, was sadly misshapen. She was brown, with skin like parchment, and piteously thin. There were lines, some deep as if old age had cut them, about the eyes and mouth.

"An' how you lef' 'em all, yonda?" she asked, in a high voice that had grown shrill from screaming at children and dogs.

"They all well. It's mighty li'le sickness in the country this yea'. But they been lookin' fo' you up yonda, straight along, Mentine."

"Don't talk, Doudouce, it's no chance; with that po' we' out piece o' lan' w'at Jules got. He say, anotha yea' like that, he's goin' sell out, him."

The children were clutching her on either side, their persistent gaze always fastened upon Doudouce. He tried without avail to make friends with them. Then Jules came home from the field, riding the mule with which he had worked, and which he fastened outside the gate.

"Yere's Doudouce f'om Natchitoches, Jules," called out Mentine, "he stop' to tell us howdy, *en passant*." The husband mounted to the gallery and the two men shook hands; Doudouce listlessly, as he had done with Mentine; Jules with some bluster and show of cordiality.

"Well, you' a lucky man, you," he exclaimed with his swagger air, "able to broad like that, *encore!* You could n't do that if you had half a dozen mouth' to feed, *allez!*"

"Non, j'te garantis!" agreed Mentine, with a loud laugh. Doudouce winced, as he had done the instant before at Jules's heartless implication. This husband of Mentine surely had not changed during the seven years, except to grow broader, stronger, handsomer. But Doudouce did not tell him so.

After the mid-day dinner of boiled salt pork, corn bread and molasses, there was nothing for Doudouce but to take his leave when Jules did.

At the gate, the little boy was discovered in dangerous proximity to the mule's heels, and was properly screamed at and rebuked.

"I reckon he likes hosses," Doudouce remarked. "He take' afta you, Mentine. I got a li'le pony yonda home," he said, addressing the child, "w'at ent ne use to me. I'm goin' sen' 'im down to you. He's a good, tough li'le mustang. You jis can let 'im eat grass an' feed 'im a ban'ful 'o co'n, once a w'ile. An' he's gentle, yes. You an' yo' ma can ride 'im to church, Sundays. *Hein!* you want?"

"W'at you say, Jules?" demanded the father. "W'at you say?" echoed Mentine, who was balancing the baby across the gate.

"'Tit sauvage, va!"

Doudouce shook hands all around, even with the baby, and walked off in the opposite direction to Jules, who had mounted the mule. He was bewildered. He stumbled over the rough ground because of tears that were blinding him, and that he had held in check for the past hour.

He had loved Mentine long ago, when she was young and attractive, and he found that he loved her still. He had tried to put all disturbing thought of her away, on that wedding-day, and he supposed he had succeeded. But he loved her now as he never had. Because she was no longer beautiful, he loved her. Because the delicate bloom of her existence had been rudely brushed away; because she was in a manner fallen; because she was Mentine, he loved her; fiercely, as a mother loves an afflicted child. He would have liked to thrust that man aside, and gather up her and her children, and hold them and keep them as long as life lasted.

After a moment or two Doudouce looked back at Mentine, standing at the gate with her baby. But her face was turned away from him. She was gazing after her husband, who went in the direction of the field.

A Wizard from Gettysburg

I t was one afternoon in April, not long ago, only the other day, and the shadows had already begun to lengthen.

Bertrand Delmandé, a fine, bright-looking boy of fourteen years,—fifteen, perhaps,—was mounted, and riding along a pleasant country road, upon a little Creole pony, such as boys in Louisiana usually ride when they have nothing better at hand. He had hunted, and carried his gun before him.

It is unpleasant to state that Bertrand was not so depressed as he should have been, in view of recent events that had come about. Within the past week he had been recalled from the college of Grand Coteau to his home, the Bon-Accueil plantation.

He had found his father and his grandmother depressed over money matters, awaiting certain legal developments that might result in his permanent withdrawal from school. That very day, directly after the early dinner, the two had driven to town, on this very business, to be absent till the late afternoon. Bertrand, then, had saddled Picayune and gone for a long jaunt, such as his heart delighted in.

He was returning now, and had approached the beginning of the great tangled Cherokee hedge that marked the boundary line of Bon-Accueil, and that twinkled with multiple white roses.

The pony started suddenly and violently at something there in the turn of the road, and just under the hedge. It looked like a bundle of rags at first. But it was a tramp, seated upon a broad, flat stone.

Bertrand had no maudlin consideration for tramps as a species; he had only that morning driven from the place one who was making himself unpleasant at the kitchen window.

But this tramp was old and feeble. His beard was long, and as white as new-ginned cotton, and when Bertrand saw him he was engaged in stanching a wound in his bare heel with a fistful of matted grass.

"What's wrong, old man?" asked the boy, kindly.

The tramp looked up at him with a bewildered glance, but did not answer.

"Well," thought Bertrand, "since it's decided that I'm to be a physician some day, I can't begin to practice too early."

He dismounted, and examined the injured foot. It had an ugly gash. Bertrand acted mostly from impulse. Fortunately his impulses were not bad ones. So, nimbly, and as quickly as he could manage it', he had the old man astride Picayune, whilst he himself was leading the pony down the narrow lane.

The dark green hedge towered like a high and solid wall on one side. On the other was a broad, open field, where here and there appeared the flash and gleam of uplifted, polished hoes, that negroes were plying between the even rows of cotton and tender corn.

"This is the State of Louisiana," uttered the tramp, quaveringly.

"Yes, this is Louisiana," returned Bertrand cheerily.

"Yes, I know it is. I've been in all of them since Gettysburg. Sometimes it was too hot, and sometimes it was too cold; and with that bullet in my head—you don't remember? No, you don't remember Gettysburg."

"Well, no, not vividly," laughed Bertrand.

"Is it a hospital? It isn't a factory, is it?" the man questioned.

"Where we 're going? Why, no, it's the Delmandé plantation—Bon-Accueil. Here we are. Wait, I 'll open the gate."

This singular group entered the yard from the rear, and not far from the house. A big black woman, who sat just without a cabin door, picking a pile of rusty-looking moss, called out at sight of them:—

"W'at's dat you's bringin' in dis yard, boy? top dat hoss?"

She received no reply. Bertrand, indeed, took no notice of her inquiry.

"Fu' a boy w'at goes to school like you does—whar's yo'sense?" she went on, with a fine show of indignation; then, muttering to herself, "Ma'ame Bertrand an' Marse St. Ange ain't gwine stan' dat, I knows dey ain't. Dah! ef he ain't done sot 'im on de gall'ry, plumb down in his pa's rockin'-cheer!"

Which the boy had done; seated the tramp in a pleasant corner of the veranda, while he went in search of bandages for his wound.

The servants showed high disapproval, the housemaid following Bertrand into his grandmother's room, whither he had carried his investigations.

"W'at you tearin' yo' gra'ma's closit to' pieces dat away, boy?" she complained in her high soprano.

"I'm looking for bandages."

"Den w'y you don't ax fu' ban'ges, an' lef yo' gra'ma's closit 'lone? You want to listen to me; you gwine git shed o' dat tramp settin' dah naxt to de dinin'-room! W'en de silva be missin', 'tain' you w'at gwine git blame, it's me."

"The silver? Nonsense, 'Cindy; the man's wounded, and can't you see he's out of his head?"

"No mo' outen his head 'an I is. 'T ain' me w'at want to tres' (trust) 'im wid de sto'-room key, ef he is outen his head," she concluded with a disdainful shrug.

But Bertrand's protégé proved so unapproachable in his long-worn rags, that the boy concluded to leave him unmolested till his father's return, and then ask permission to turn the forlorn creature into the bath-house, and array him afterward in clean, fresh garments.

So there the old tramp sat in the veranda corner, stolidly content, when St. Ange Delmandé and his mother returned from town.

St. Ange was a dark, slender man of middle age, with a sensitive face, and a plentiful sprinkle of gray in his thick black hair; his mother, a portly woman, and an active one for her sixty-five years.

They were evidently in a despondent mood. Perhaps it was for the cheer of her sweet presence that they had brought with them from town a little girl, the child of Madame Delmandé's only daughter, who was married, and lived there.

Madame Delmandé and her son were astonished to find so uninviting an intruder in possession. But a few earnest words from Bertrand reassured them, and partly reconciled them to the man's presence; and it was with wholly indifferent though not unkindly glances that they passed him by when they entered. On any large plantation there are always nooks and corners where, for a night or more, even such a man as this tramp may be tolerated and given shelter.

When Bertrand went to bed that night, he lay long awake thinking of the man, and of what he had heard from his lips in the hushed starlight. The boy had heard of the awfulness of Gettysburg, till it was like something he could feel and quiver at.

On that field of battle this man had received a new and tragic birth. For all his existence that went before was a blank to him. There, in the black desolation of war, he was born again, without friends or kindred; without even a name he could know was his own. Then he had gone forth a wanderer; living more than half the time in hospitals; toiling when he could, starving when he had to.

Strangely enough, he had addressed Bertrand as "St. Ange," not once, but every time he had spoken to him. The boy wondered at this. Was it because he had heard Madame Delmandé address her son by that name, and fancied it?

So this nameless wanderer had drifted far down to the plantation of Bon-Accueil, and at last had found a human hand stretched out to him in kindness.

When the family assembled at breakfast on the following morning, the tramp was already settled in the chair, and in the corner which Bertrand's indulgence had made familiar to him.

If he had turned partly around, he would have faced the flower garden, with its graveled walks and trim parterres, where a tangle of color and perfume were holding high revelry this April morning; but he liked better to gaze into the back yard, where there was always movement: men and women coming and going, bearing implements of work; little negroes in scanty garments, darting here and there, and kicking up the dust in their exuberance.

Madame Delmandé could just catch a glimpse of him through the long window that opened to the floor, and near which he sat.

Mr. Delmandé had spoken to the man pleasantly; but he and his mother were wholly absorbed by their trouble, and talked constantly of that, while Bertrand went back and forth ministering to the old man's wants. The boy knew that the servants would have done the office with ill grace, and he chose to be cup-bearer himself to the unfortunate creature for whose presence he alone was responsible.

Once, when Bertrand went out to him with a second cup of coffee, steaming and fragrant, the old man whispered:—

"What are they saying in there?" pointing over his shoulder to the dining-room.

"Oh, money troubles that will force us to economize for a while," answered the boy. "What father and *mé-mère* feel worst about is that I shall have to leave college now."

"No, no! St. Ange must go to school. The war's over, the war's over! St. Ange and Florentine must go to school."

"But if there's no money," the boy insisted, smiling like one who humors the vagaries of a child.

"Money! money!" murmured the tramp. "The war's over—money! money!"

His sleepy gaze had swept across the yard into the thick of the orchard beyond, and rested there.

Suddenly he pushed aside the light table that had been set before him, and rose, clutching Bertrand's arm.

"St. Ange, you must go to school!" he whispered. "The war's over," looking furtively around. "Come. Don't let them hear you. Don't let the negroes see us. Get a spade—the little spade that Buck Williams was digging his cistern with."

Still clutching the boy, he dragged him down the steps as he said this, and traversed the yard with long, limping strides, himself leading the way.

From under a shed where such things were to be found, Bertrand selected a spade, since the tramp's whim demanded that he should, and together they entered the orchard.

The grass was thick and tufted here, and wet with the morning dew. In long lines, forming pleasant avenues between, were peach-trees growing, and pear and apple and plum. Close against the fence was the pome-granate hedge, with its waxen blossoms, brick-red. Far down in the centre of the orchard stood a huge pecan-tree, twice the size of any other that was there, seeming to rule like an old-time king.

Here Bertrand and his guide stopped. The tramp had not once hesitated in his movements since grasping the arm of his young companion on the veranda. Now he went and leaned his back against the pecan-tree, where there was a deep knot, and looking steadily before him he took ten paces forward. Turning sharply to the right, he made five additional paces. Then pointing his finger downward, and looking at Bertrand, he commanded:—

"There, dig. I would do it myself, but for my wounded foot. For I've turned many a spade of earth since Gettysburg. Dig, St. Ange, dig! The war's over; you must go to school."

Is there a boy of fifteen under the sun who would not have dug, even knowing he was following the insane dictates of a demented man? Bertrand entered with all the zest of his years and his spirit into the curious adventure; and he dug and dug, throwing great spadefuls of the rich, fragrant earth from side to side.

The tramp, with body bent, and fingers like claws clasping his bony knees, stood watching with eager eyes, that never unfastened their steady gaze from the boy's rhythmic motions.

"That's it!" he muttered at intervals. "Dig, dig! The war's over. You must go to school, St. Ange."

Deep down in the earth, too deep for any ordinary turning of the soil with spade or plow to have reached it, was a box. It was of tin, apparently, something larger than a cigar box, and bound round and round with twine, rotted now and eaten away in places.

The tramp showed no surprise at seeing it there; he simply knelt upon the ground and lifted it from its long resting place.

Bertrand had let the spade fall from his hands, and was quivering with the awe of the thing he saw. Who could this wizard be that had come to him in the guise of a tramp, that walked in cabalistic paces upon his own father's ground, and pointed his finger like a divining-rod to the spot where boxes—may be treasures—lay? It was like a page from a wonder-book.

And walking behind this white-haired old man, who was again leading the way, something of childish superstition crept back into Bertrand's heart. It was the same feeling with which he had often sat, long ago, in the weird firelight of some negro's cabin, listening to tales of witches who came in the night to work uncanny spells at their will.

Madame Delmandé had never abandoned the custom of washing her own silver and dainty china. She sat, when the breakfast was over, with a pail of warm suds before her that 'Cindy had brought to her, with an abundance of soft linen cloths. Her little granddaughter stood beside her playing, as babies will, with the bright spoons and forks, and ranging them in rows on the polished mahogany. St. Ange was at the window making entries in a note-book, and frowning gloomily as he did so.

The group in the dining-room were so em-ployed when the old tramp came staggering in, Bertrand close behind him.

He went and stood at the foot of the table, opposite to where Madame Delmandé sat, and let fall the box upon it.

The thing in falling shattered, and from its bursting sides gold came, clicking, spinning, gliding, some of it like oil; rolling along the table and off it to the floor, but heaped up, the bulk of it, before the tramp.

"Here's money!" he called out, plunging his old hand in the thick of it. "Who says St. Ange shall not go to school? The war's over—here's money! St. Ange, my boy," turning to Bertrand and speaking with quick authority, "tell Buck Williams to hitch Black Bess to the buggy, and go bring Judge Parkerson here."

Judge Parkerson, indeed, who had been dead for twenty years and more!

"Tell him that—that"—and the hand that was not in the gold went up to the withered forehead, "that—Bertrand Delmandé needs him!"

Madame Delmandé, at sight of the man with his box and his gold, had given a sharp cry, such as might follow the plunge of a knife. She lay now in her son's arms, panting hoarsely.

"Your father, St. Ange,—come back from the dead—your father!"

"Be calm, mother!" the man implored. "You had such sure proof of his death in that terrible battle, this *may* not be he."

"I know him! I know your father, my son!" and disengaging herself from the arms that held her, she dragged herself as a wounded serpent might to where the old man stood.

His hand was still in the gold, and on his face was yet the flush which had come there when he shouted out the name Bertrand Delmandé.

"Husband," she gasped, "do you know me—your wife?"

The little girl was playing gleefully with the yellow coin.

Bertrand stood, pulseless almost, like a young Actæon cut in marble.

When the old man had looked long into the woman's imploring face, he made a courtly-bow.

"Madame," he said, "an old soldier, wounded on the field of Gettysburg, craves for himself and his two little children your kind hospitality."

MA'AME PÉLAGIE

I

WHEN THE WAR BEGAN, THERE stood on Côte Joyeuse an imposing mansion of red brick, shaped like the Pantheon. A grove of majestic live-oaks surrounded it.

Thirty years later, only the thick walls were standing, with the dull red brick showing here and there through a matted growth of clinging vines. The huge round pillars were intact; so to some extent was the stone flagging of hall and portico. There had been no home so stately along the whole stretch of Côte Joyeuse. Every one knew that, as they knew it had cost Philippe Valmet sixty thousand dollars to build, away back in 1840. No one was in danger of forgetting that fact, so long as his daughter Pélagie survived. She was a queenly, white-haired woman of fifty. "Ma'ame Pélagie," they called her, though she was unmarried, as was her sister Pauline, a child in Ma'ame Pélagie's eyes; a child of thirty-five. The two lived alone in a three-roomed cabin, almost within the shadow of the ruin. They lived for a dream, for Ma'ame Pélagie's dream, which was to rebuild the old home.

It would be pitiful to tell how their days were spent to accomplish this end; how the dollars had been saved for thirty years and the picayunes hoarded; and yet, not half enough gathered! But Ma'ame Pélagie felt sure of twenty years of life before her, and counted upon as many more for her sister. And what could not come to pass in twenty—in forty—years?

Often, of pleasant afternoons, the two would drink their black coffee, seated upon the stone-flagged portico whose canopy was the blue sky of Louisiana. They loved to sit there in the silence, with only each other and the sheeny, prying lizards for company, talking of the old times and planning for the new; while light breezes stirred the tattered vines high up among the columns, where owls nested.

"We can never hope to have all just as it was, Pauline," Ma'ame Pélagie would say; "perhaps the marble pillars of the salon will have to be replaced by wooden ones, and the crystal candelabra left out. Should you be willing, Pauline?"

"Oh, yes, Sesœur, I shall be willing." It was always, "Yes, Sesœur," or "No, Sesœur," "Just as you please, Sesœur," with poor little Mam'selle Pauline. For what did she remember of that old life and that old

KATE CHOPIN

splendor? Only a faint gleam here and there; the half-consciousness of a young, uneventful existence; and then a great crash. That meant the nearness of war; the revolt of slaves; confusion ending in fire and flame through which she was borne safely in the strong arms of Pélagie, and carried to the log cabin which was still their home. Their brother, Léandre, had known more of it all than Pauline, and not so much as Pélagie. He had left the management of the big plantation with all its memories and traditions to his older sister, and had gone away to dwell in cities. That was many years ago. Now, Léandre's business called him frequently and upon long journeys from home, and his motherless daughter was coming to stay with her aunts at Côte Joyeuse.

They talked about it, sipping their coffee on the ruined portico. Mam'selle Pauline was terribly excited; the flush that throbbed into her pale, nervous face showed it; and she locked her thin fingers in and out incessantly.

"But what shall we do with La Petite, Sesœur? Where shall we put her? How shall we amuse her? Ah, Seigneur!"

"She will sleep upon a cot in the room next to ours," responded Ma'ame Pélagie, "and live as we do. She knows how we live, and why we live; her father has told her. She knows we have money and could squander it if we chose. Do not fret, Pauline; let us hope La Petite is a true Valmet."

Then Ma'ame Pélagie rose with stately deliberation and went to saddle? her horse, for she had yet to make her last daily round through the fields; and Mam'selle Pauline threaded her way slowly among the tangled grasses toward the cabin.

The coming of La Petite, bringing with her as she did the pungent atmosphere of an outside and dimly known world, was a shock to these two, lining their dream-life. The girl was quite as tall as her aunt Pélagie, with dark eyes that reflected joy as a still pool reflects the light of stars; and her rounded cheek was tinged like the pink crèpe myrtle. Mam'selle Pauline kissed her and trembled. Ma'ame Pélagie looked into her eyes with a searching gaze, which seemed to seek a likeness of the past in the living present.

And they made room between them for this young life.

II

La Petite had determined upon trying to fit herself to the strange, narrow existence which she knew awaited her at Côte Joyeuse.

It went well enough at first. Sometimes she followed Ma'ame Pélagie into the fields to note how the cotton was opening, ripe and white; or to count the ears of corn upon the hardy stalks. But oftener she was with her aunt Pauline, assisting in household offices, chattering of her brief past, or walking with the older woman arm-in-arm under the trailing moss of the giant oaks.

Mam'selle Pauline's steps grew very buoy-ant that summer, and her eyes were sometimes as bright as a bird's, unless La Petite were away from her side, when they would lose all other light but one of uneasy expectancy. The girl seemed to love her well in return, and called her endearingly Tan'-tante. But as the time went by, La Petite became very quiet,—not listless, but thoughtful, and slow in her movements. Then her cheeks began to pale, till they were tinged like the creamy plumes of the white crêpe myrtle that grew in the ruin.

One day when she sat within its shadow, between her aunts, holding a hand of each, she said: "Tante Pélagie, I must tell you something, you and Tan'tante." She spoke low, but clearly and firmly. "I love you both,— please remember that I love you both. But I must go away from you. I can't live any longer here at Côte Joyeuse."

A spasm passed through Mam'selle Pauline's delicate frame. La Petite could feel the twitch of it in the wiry fingers that were intertwined with her own. Ma'ame Pélagie remained unchanged and motionless. No human eye could penetrate so deep as to see the satisfaction which her soul felt. She said: "What do you mean, Petite? Your father has sent you to us, and I am sure it is his wish that you remain."

"My father loves me, tante Pélagie, and such will not be his wish when he knows. Oh!" she continued with a restless movement, "it is as though a weight were pressing me backward here. I must live another life; the life I lived before. I want to know things that are happening from day to day over the world, and hear them talked about. I want my music, my books, my companions. If I had known no other life but this one of privation, I suppose it would be different. If I had to live this life, I should make the best of it. But I do not have to; and you know, tante Pélagie, you do not need to. It seems to me," she added in a whisper, "that it is a sin against myself. Ah, Tan'tante!—what is the matter with Tan'tante?"

It was nothing; only a slight feeling of faintness, that would soon pass. She entreated them to take no notice; but they brought her some water and fanned her with a palmetto leaf.

But that night, in the stillness of the room, Mam'selle Pauline sobbed and would not be comforted. Ma'ame Pélagie took her in her arms.

"Pauline, my little sister Pauline," she entreated, "I never have seen you like this before. Do you no longer love me? Have we not been happy together, you and I?"

"Oh, yes, Sesœur."

"Is it because La Petite is going away?"

"Yes, Sesœur."

"Then she is dearer to you than I!" spoke Ma'ame Pélagie with sharp resentment. "Than I, who held you and warmed you in my arms the day you were born; than I, your mother, father, sister, everything that could cherish you. Pauline, don't tell me that."

Mam'selle Pauline tried to talk through her sobs.

"I can't explain it to you, Sesœur. I don't understand it myself. I love you as I have always loved you; next to God. But if La Petite goes away I shall die. I can't understand,—help me, Sesœur. She seems—she seems like a saviour; like one who had come and taken me by the hand and was leading me somewhere—somewhere I want to go."

Ma'ame Pélagie had been sitting beside the bed in her peignoir and slippers. She held the hand of her sister who lay there, and smoothed down the woman's soft brown hair. She said not a! word, and the silence was broken only by Ma'mselle Pauline's continued sobs. Once Ma'ame Pélagie arose to drink of orange-flower water, which she gave to her sister, as she would have offered it to a nervous, fretful child. Almost an hour passed before Ma'ame Pélagie spoke again. Then she said:—

"Pauline, you must cease that sobbing, now, and sleep. You will make yourself ill. La Petite will not go away. Do you hear me? Do you understand? She will stay, I promise you."

Mam'selle Pauline could not clearly comprehend, but she had great faith in the word of her sister, and soothed by the promise and the touch of Ma'ame Pélagie's strong, gentle hand, she fell asleep.

III

MA'AME PÉLAGIE, WHEN SHE SAW that her sister slept, arose noiselessly and stepped outside upon the low-roofed narrow gallery. She did not linger there, but with a step that was hurried and agitated, she crossed the distance that divided her cabin from the ruin.

The night was not a dark one, for the sky was clear and the moon resplendent. But light or dark would have made no difference to Ma'ame Pélagie. It was not the first time she had stolen away to the ruin at night-time, when the whole plantation slept; but she never before had been there with a heart so nearly broken. She was going there for the last time to dream her dreams; to see the visions that hitherto had crowded her days and nights, and to bid them farewell.

There was the first of them, awaiting her upon the very portal; a robust old white-haired man, chiding her for returning home so late. There are guests to be entertained. Does she not know it? Guests from the city and from the near plantations. Yes, she knows it is late. She had been abroad with Félix, and they did not notice how the time was speeding. Félix is there; he will explain it all. He is there beside her, but she does not want to hear what he will tell her father.

Ma'ame Pélagie had sunk upon the bench where she and her sister so often came to sit. Turning, she gazed in through the gaping chasm of the window at her side. The interior of the ruin is ablaze. Not with the moonlight, for that is faint beside the other one—the sparkle from the crystal candelabra, which negroes, moving noiselessly and respectfully about, are lighting, one after the other. How the gleam of them reflects and glances from the polished marble pillars!

The room holds a number of guests. There is old Monsieur Lucien Santien, leaning against one of the pillars, and laughing at something which Monsieur Lafirme is telling him, till his fat shoulders shake. His son Jules is with him—Jules, who wants to marry her. She laughs. She wonders if Félix has told her father yet. There is young Jerome Lafirme playing at checkers upon the sofa with Léandre. Little Pauline stands annoying them and disturbing the game. Léandre reproves her. She begins to cry, and old black Clémentine, her nurse, who is not far off, limps across the room to pick her up and carry her away. How sensitive the little one is! But she trots about and takes care of herself better than she did a year or two ago, when she fell upon the stone hall floor and raised a great "bo-bo" on her forehead. Pélagie was hurt and angry enough about it; and she ordered rugs and buffalo robes to be brought and laid thick upon the tiles, till the little one's steps were surer.

"Il ne faut pas faire mal à Pauline."

She was saying it aloud—"faire mal à Pauline."

But she gazes beyond the salon, back into the big dining hall, where the white crèpe myrtle grows. Ha! how low that bat has circled. It has struck Ma'ame Pélagie full on the breast. She does not know it. She is beyond there in the dining hall, where her father sits with a group of friends over their wine. As usual they are talking politics. How tiresome! She has heard them say "la guerre" oftener than once. La guerre. Bah! She and Félix have something pleasanter to talk about, out under the oaks, or back in the shadow of the oleanders.

But they were right! The sound of a cannon, shot at Sumter, has rolled across the' Southern States, and its echo is heard along the whole stretch of Côte Joyeuse.

Yet Pélagie does not believe it. Not till La Ricaneuse stands before her with bare, black arms akimbo, uttering a volley of vile abuse and of brazen impudence. Pélagie wants to kill her. But yet she will not believe. Not till Félix comes to her in the chamber above the dining hall—there where that trumpet vine hangs—comes to say good-by to her. The hurt which the big brass buttons of his new gray uniform pressed into the tender flesh of her bosom has never left it. She sits upon the sofa, and he beside her, both speechless with pain. That room would not have been altered. Even the sofa would have been there in the same spot, and Ma'ame Pélagie had meant all along, for thirty years, all along, to lie there upon it some day when the time came to die.

But there is no time to weep, with the enemy at the door. The door has been no barrier. They are clattering through the halls now, drinking the wines, shattering the crystal and glass, slashing the portraits.

One of them stands before her and tells her to leave the house. She slaps his face. How the stigma stands out red as blood upon his blanched cheek!

Now there is a roar of fire and the flames are bearing down upon her motionless figure. She wants to show them how a daughter of Louisiana can perish before her conquerors. But little Pauline clings to her knees in an agony of terror. Little Pauline must be saved.

"Il ne faut pas faire mal à Pauline."

Again she is saying it aloud—"faire mal à Pauline."

THE NIGHT WAS NEARLY SPENT; Ma'ame Pélagie had glided from the bench upon which she had rested, and for hours lay prone upon the stone flagging, motionless. When she dragged herself to her feet it was to walk like one in a dream. About the great, solemn pillars, one after the other, she reached her arms, and pressed her cheek and her lips upon the senseless brick.

"Adieu, adieu!" whispered Ma'ame Pélagie.

There was no longer the moon to guide her steps across the familiar pathway to the cabin. The brightest light in the sky was Venus, that swung low in the east. The bats had ceased to beat their wings about the ruin. Even the mocking-bird that had warbled for hours in the old mulberry-tree had sung himself asleep. That darkest hour before the day was mantling the earth. Ma'ame Pélagie hurried through the wet, clinging grass, beating aside the heavy moss that swept across her face, walking on toward the cabin—toward Pauline. Not once did she look back upon the ruin that brooded like a huge monster—a black spot in the darkness that enveloped it.

IV

LITTLE MORE THAN A YEAR later the transformation which the old Valmet place had undergone was the talk and wonder of Côte Joyeuse. One would have looked in vain for the ruin; it was no longer there; neither was the log cabin. But out in the open, where the sun shone upon it, and the breezes blew about it, was a shapely structure fashioned from woods that the forests of the State had furnished. It rested upon a solid foundation of brick.

Upon a corner of the pleasant gallery sat Léandre smoking his afternoon cigar, and chatting with neighbors who had called. This was to be his *pied à terre* now; the home where his sisters and his daughter dwelt. The laughter of young people was heard out under the trees, and within the house where La Petite was playing upon the piano. With the enthusiasm of a young artist she drew from the keys strains that seemed marvelously beautiful to Mam'selle Pauline, who stood enraptured near her. Mam'selle Pauline had been touched by the re-creation of Valmet. Her cheek was as full and almost as flushed as La Petite's. The years were falling away from her.

Ma'ame Pélagie had been conversing with her brother and his friends. Then she turned and walked away; stopping to listen awhile to the music which La Petite was making. But it was only for a moment. She went on around the curve of the veranda, where she found herself alone. She stayed there, erect, holding to the banister rail and looking out calmly in the distance across the fields.

She was dressed in black, with the white kerchief she always wore folded across her bosom. Her thick, glossy hair rose like a silver diadem from her brow. In her deep, dark eyes smouldered the light of fires that would never flame. She had grown very old. Years instead of months seemed to have passed over her since the night she bade farewell to her visions.

Poor Ma'ame Pélagie! How could it be different! While the outward pressure of a young and joyous existence had forced her footsteps into the light, her soul had stayed in the shadow of the ruin.

At the 'Cadian Ball

Bobinôt, that big, brown, good-natured Bobinôt, had no intention of going to the ball, even though he knew Calixta would be there. For what came of those balls but heartache, and a sickening disinclination for work the whole week through, till Saturday night came again and his tortures began afresh? Why could he not love Ozéina, who would marry him to-morrow; or Fronie, or any one of a dozen others, rather than that little Spanish vixen? Calixta's slender foot had never touched Cuban soil; but her mother's had, and the Spanish was in her blood all the same. For that reason the prairie people forgave her much that they would not have overlooked in their own daughters or sisters.

Her eyes,—Bobinôt thought of her eyes, and weakened,—the bluest, the drowsiest, most tantalizing that ever looked into a man's; he thought of her flaxen hair that kinked worse than a mulatto's close to her head; that broad, smiling mouth and tip-tilted nose, that full figure; that voice like a rich contralto song, with cadences in it that must have been taught by Satan, for there was no one else to teach her tricks on that 'Cadian prairie. Bobinôt thought of them all as he plowed his rows of cane.

There had even been a breath of scandal whispered about her a year ago, when she went to Assumption,—but why talk of it? No one did now. "C'est Espagnol, ça," most of them said with lenient shoulder-shrugs. "Bon chien tient de race," the old men mumbled over their pipes, stirred by recollections. Nothing was made of it, except that Fronie threw it up to Calixta when the two quarreled and fought on the church steps after mass one Sunday, about a lover. Calixta swore roundly in fine 'Cadian French and with true Spanish spirit, and slapped Fronie's face. Fronie had slapped her back; "Tiens, bocotte, va!" "Espèce de lionèse; prends ça, et ça!" till the curé himself was obliged to hasten and make peace between them. Bobinôt thought of it all, and would not go to the ball.

But in the afternoon, over at Friedheimer's store, where he was buying a trace-chain, he heard some one say that Alcée Laballière would be there. Then wild horses could not have kept him away. He knew how it would be—or rather he did not know how it would be—if the handsome young planter came over to the ball as he sometimes did. If Alcée happened to be in a serious mood, he might only go to the card-room and play a round or two; or he might stand out on the galleries talking crops and politics with the old people. But there was po telling. A drink or two could put the devil in his head,—that was what Bobinôt said to himself, as he wiped the sweat from his brow with his red bandanna; a gleam from Calixta's eyes, a flash of her ankle, a twirl of her skirts could do the same. Yes, Bobinôt would go to the ball.

THAT WAS THE YEAR ALCÉE Laballière put nine hundred acres in rice. It was putting a good deal of money into the ground, but the returns promised to be glorious. Old Madame Laballière, sailing about the spacious galleries in her white *volante*, figured it all out in her head. Clarisse, her god-daughter, helped her a little, and together they built more air-castles than enough. Alcée worked like a mule that time; and if he did not kill himself, it was because his constitution was an iron one. It was an every-day affair for him to come in from the field well-nigh exhausted, and wet to the waist. He did not mind if there were visitors; he left them to his mother and Clarisse. There were often guests: young men and women who came up from the city, which was but a few hours away, to visit his beautiful kinswoman. She was worth going a good deal farther than that to see. Dainty as a lily; hardy as a sunflower; slim, tall, graceful, like one of the reeds that grew in the marsh. Cold and kind and cruel by turn, and everything that was aggravating to Alcée.

He would have liked to sweep the place of those visitors, often. Of the men, above all, with their ways and their manners; their swaying of fans like women, and dandling about hammocks. He could have pitched them over the levee into the river, if it hadn't meant murder. That was Alcée. But he must have been crazy the day he came in from the rice-field, and, toil-stained as he was, clasped Clarisse by the arms and panted a volley of hot, blistering love-words into her face. No man had ever spoken love to her like that.

"Monsieur!" she exclaimed, looking him full in the eyes, without a quiver. Alcée's hands dropped and his glance wavered before the chill of her calm, clear eyes.

"*Par exemple!*" she muttered disdainfully, as she turned from him, deftly adjusting the careful toilet that he had so brutally disarranged.

That happened a day or two before the cyclone came that cut into the rice like fine steel. It was an awful thing, coming so swiftly, without a moment's warning in which to light a holy candle or set a piece of blessed palm burning. Old madame wept openly and said her beads, just as her son Didier, the New Orleans one, would have done. If such a thing had happened to Alphonse, the Laballière planting cotton up in Natchitoches, he would have raved and stormed like a second cyclone, and made his surroundings unbearable for a day or two. But Alcée took the misfortune differently. He looked ill and gray after it, and said nothing. His speechlessness was frightful. Clarisse's heart melted with tenderness; but when she offered her soft, purring words of condolence, he accepted them with mute indifference. Then she and her nénaine wept afresh in each other's arms.

A night or two later, when Clarisse went to her window to kneel there in the moonlight and say her prayers before retiring, she saw that Bruce, Alcée's negro servant, had led his master's saddle-horse noiselessly along the edge of the sward that bordered the gravel-path, and stood holding him near by. Presently, she heard Alcée quit his room, which was beneath her own, and traverse the lower portico. As he emerged from the shadow and crossed the strip of moonlight, she perceived that he carried a pair of well-filled saddle-bags which he at once flung across the animal's back. He then lost no time in mounting, and after a brief exchange of words with Bruce, went cantering away, taking no precaution to avoid the noisy gravel as the negro had done.

Clarisse had never Suspected that it might be Alcée's custom to sally forth from the plantation secretly, and at such an hour; for it was nearly midnight. And had it not been for the telltale saddle-bags, she would only have crept to bed, to wonder, to fret and dream unpleasant dreams. But her impatience and anxiety would not be held in check. Hastily unbolting the shutters of her door that opened upon the gallery, she stepped outside and called softly to the old negro.

"Gre't Peter! Miss Clarisse. I was n' sho it was a ghos' o' w'at, stan'in' up dah, plumb in de night, data way."

He mounted halfway up the long, broad flight of stairs. She was standing at the top.

"Bruce, w'ere has Monsieur Alcée gone?" she asked.

"W'y, he gone 'bout he business, I reckin," replied Bruce, striving to be non-committal at the outset.

"W'ere has Monsieur Alcée gone?" she reiterated, stamping her bare foot. "I won't stan' any nonsense or any lies; mine, Bruce."

"I don' ric'lie ez I eva tole you lie *yit*, Miss Clarisse. Mista Alcée, he all broke up, sho."

"W'ere—has—he gone? Ah, Sainte Vierge! faut de la patience! butor, va!"

"W'en I was in he room, a-breshin' off he clo'es to-day," the darkey began, settling himself against the stair-rail, "he look dat speechless an' down, I say, 'You 'pear tu me like some pussun w'at gwine have a spell o' sickness, Mista Alcée.' He say, 'You reckin?' 'I dat he git up, go look hisse'f stiddy in de glass. Den he go to de chimbly an' jerk up de quinine bottle an po' a gre't hoss-dose on to be ban'. An' he swalla dat mess in a wink, an' wash hit down wid a big dram o' w'iskey w'at he keep in he room, aginst he come all soppin' wet outen de fiel'.

"He 'lows, 'No, I ain' gwine be sick, Bruce.' Den he square off. He say, 'I kin mak out to stan' up an' gi' an' take wid any man I knows, lessen hit's John L. Sulvun. But w'en God A'mighty an' a 'oman jines fo'ces agin me, dat's one too many fur me.' I tell 'im, 'Jis so,' whils' I'se makin' out to bresh a spot off w'at ain' dah, on he coat colla. I tell 'im, 'You wants li'le res', suh.' He say, 'No, I wants li'le fling; dat w'at I wants; an I gwine git it. Pitch me a fis'ful o' clo'es in dem 'ar saddle-bags.' Dat w'at he say. Don't you bodda, missy. He jis' gone a-caperin' yonda to de Cajun ball. Uh—uh—de skeeters is fair' a-swarmin' like bees roun' yo' foots!"

The mosquitoes were indeed attacking Clarisse's white feet savagely. She had unconsciously been alternately rubbing one foot over the other during the darkey's recital.

"The 'Cadian ball," she repeated contemptuously. "Humph! *Par exemple!* Nice conduc' for a Laballière. An' he needs a saddle-bag, fill' with clothes, to go to the 'Cadian ball!"

"Oh, Miss Clarisse; you go on to bed, chile; git yo' soun' sleep. He 'low he come back in couple weeks o' so. I kiarn be repeatin' lot o' truck w'at young mans say, out heah face o' a young gal."

Clarisse said no more, but turned and abruptly reëntered the house.

"You done talk too much wid yo' mouf a'ready, you ole fool nigga, you," muttered Bruce to himself as he walked away.

ALCÉE REACHED THE BALL VERY late, of course—too late for the chicken gumbo which had been served at midnight.

The big, low-ceiled room—they called it a hall—was packed with men and women dancing to the music of three fiddles. There were broad galleries all around it. There was a room at one side where sober-faced men were playing cards. Another, in which babies were sleeping, was called *le parc aux petits.* Any one who is white may go to a 'Cadian ball, but he must pay for his lemonade, his coffee and chicken gumbo.

And he must behave himself like a 'Cadian. Grosbœuf was giving this ball. He had been giving them since he was a young man, and he was a middle-aged one, now. In that time he could recall but one disturbance, and that was caused by American railroaders, who were not in touch with their surroundings and had no business there. "Ces maudits gens du raiderode," Grosbœuf called them.

Alcée Laballière's presence at the ball caused a flutter even among the men, who could not but admire his "nerve" after such misfortune befalling him. To be sure, they knew the Laballières were rich—that there were resources East, and more again in the city. But they felt it took a brave homme to stand a blow like that philosophically. One old gentleman, who was in the habit of reading a Paris newspaper and knew things, chuckled gleefully to, everybody that Alcée's conduct was altogether chic, mais chic. That he had more *panache* than Boulanger. Well, perhaps he had.

But what he did not show outwardly was that he was in a mood for ugly things to-night. Poor Bobinôt alone felt it vaguely. He discerned a gleam of it in Alcée's handsome eyes, as the young planter stood in the doorway, looking with rather feverish glance upon the assembly, while he laughed and talked with a 'Cadian farmer who was beside him.

Bobinôt himself was dull-looking and clumsy. Most of the men were. But the young women were very beautiful. The eyes that glanced into Alcée's as they passed him were big, dark, soft as those of the young heifers standing out in the cool prairie grass.

But the belle was Calixta. Her white dress was not nearly so handsome or well made as Fronie's (she and Fronie had quite forgotten the battle on the church steps, and were friends again), nor were her slippers so stylish as those of Ozéina; and she fanned herself with a handkerchief, since she had broken her red fan at the last ball, and her aunts and uncles were not willing to give her another. But all the men agreed she was at her best to-night. Such animation! and abandon! such flashes of wit!

"He, Bobinôt! *Mais* w'at's the matta? W'at you standin' *planté là* like ole Ma'ame Tina's cow in the bog, you?"

That was good. That was an excellent thrust at Bobinôt, who had forgotten the figure of the dance with his mind bent on other things, and it started a clamor of laughter at his expense. He joined good-naturedly. It was better to receive even such notice as that from Calixta than none at all. But Madame Suzonne, sitting in a corner, whispered to her neighbor that if Ozéina were to conduct herself in a like manner, she should immediately be taken out to the mule-cart and driven home. The women did not always approve of Calixta.

Now and then were short lulls in the dance, when couples flocked out upon the galleries for a brief respite and fresh air. The moon had gone down pale in the west, and in the east was yet no promise of day. After such an interval, when the dancers again assembled to resume the interrupted quadrille, Calixta was not among them.

She was sitting upon a bench out in the shadow, with Alcée beside her. They were acting like fools. He had attempted to take a little gold ring from her finger; just for the fun of it, for there was nothing he could have done with the ring but replace it again. But she clinched her hand tight. He pretended that it was a very difficult matter to open it. Then he kept the hand in his. They seemed to forget about it. He played with her ear-ring, a thin crescent of gold hanging from her small brown ear. He caught a wisp of the kinky hair that had escaped its fastening, and rubbed the ends of it against his shaven cheek.

"You know, last year in Assumption, Calixta?" They belonged to the younger generation, so preferred to speak English.

"Don't come say Assumption to me, M'sieur Alcée. I done yeard Assumption till I'm plumb sick."

"Yes, I know. The idiots! Because you were in Assumption, and I happened to go to Assumption, they must have it that we went together. But it was nice—*hein*, Calixta?—in Assumption?"

They saw Bobinôt emerge from the hall and stand a moment outside the lighted doorway, peering uneasily and searchingly into the darkness. He did not see them, and went slowly back.

"There is Bobinôt looking for you. You are going to set poor Bobinôt crazy. You'll marry him some day; *hein*, Calixta?"

"I don't say no, me," she replied, striving to withdraw her hand, which he held more, firmly for the attempt.

"But come, Calixta; you know you said you would go back to Assumption, just to spite them."

"No, I neva said that, me. You mus' dreamt that."

"Oh, I thought you did. You know I'm going down to the city."

"W'en?"

"To-night."

"Betta make has'e, then; it's mos' day."

"Well, to-morrow'll do."

"W'at you goin' do, yonda?"

"I don't know. Drown myself in the lake, maybe; unless you go down there to visit your uncle."

Calixta's senses were reeling; and they well-nigh left her when she felt Alcée's lips brush her ear like the touch of a rose.

"Mista Alcée! Is dat Mista Alcée?" the thick voice of a negro was asking; he stood on the ground, holding to the banister-rails near which the couple sat.

"W'at do you want now?" cried Alcée impatiently. "Can't I have a moment of peace?"

"I ben huntin' you high an' low, suh," answered the man. "Dey—dey some one in de road, onda de mulbare-tree, want see you a minute."

"I would n't go out to the road to see the Angel Gabriel. And if you come back here with any more talk, I 'll have to break your neck." The negro turned mumbling away.

Alcée and Calixta laughed softly about it. Her boisterousness was all gone. They talked low, and laughed softly, as lovers do.

"Alcée! Alcée Laballière!"

It was not the negro's voice this time; but one that went through Alcée's body like an electric shock, bringing him to his feet.

Clarisse was standing there in her riding-habit, where the negro had stood. For an instant confusion reigned in Alcée's thoughts, as with one who awakes suddenly from a dream. But he felt that something of serious import had brought his cousin to the ball in the dead of night.

"W'at does this mean, Clarisse?" he asked.

"It means something has happen' at home. You mus' come."

"Happened to maman?" he questioned, in alarm.

"No; nénaine is well, and asleep. It is something else. Not to frighten you. But you mus' come. Come with me, Alcée."

There was no need for the imploring note. He would have followed the voice anywhere.

She had now recognized the girl sitting back on the bench.

"Ah, c'est vous, Calixta? Comment ça va, mon enfant?"

"Tcha va b'en; et vous, mam'zélle?"

Alcée swung himself over the low rail and started to follow Clarisse, without a word, without a glance back at the girl. He had forgotten he was leaving her there. But Clarisse whispered something to him, and he turned back to say "Good-night, Calixta," and offer his hand to press through the railing. She pretended not to see it.

"How come that? You settin' yere by yo'se'f, Calixta?" It was Bobinôt who had found her there alone. The dancers had not yet come out. She looked ghastly in the faint, gray light struggling out of the east.

"Yes, that's me. Go yonda in the *parc aux petits* an' ask Aunt Olisse fu' my hat. She knows w'ere 't is. I want to go home, me."

"How you came?"

"I come afoot, with the Cateaus. But I'm goin' now. I ent goin' wait fu' 'em. I'm plumb we' out, me."

"Kin I go with you, Calixta?"

"I don' care."

They went together across the open prairie and along the edge of the fields, stumbling in the uncertain light. He told her to lift her dress that was getting wet and bedraggled; for she was pulling at the weeds and grasses with her hands.

"I don' care; it's got to go in the tub, anyway. You been say in' all along you want to marry me, Bobinôt. Well, if you want, yet, I don' care, me."

The glow of a sudden and overwhelming happiness shone out in the brown, rugged face of the young Acadian. He could not speak, for very joy. It choked him.

"Oh well, if you don' want," snapped Calixta, flippantly, pretending to be piqued at his silence.

"*Bon Dieu!* You know that makes me crazy, w'at you sayin'. You mean that, Calixta? You ent goin' turn roun' agin?"

"I neva tole you that much *yet*, Bobinôt. I mean that. *Tiens*," and she held out her hand in the business-like manner of a man who clinches a bargain with a hand-clasp. Bobinôt grew bold with happiness and asked Calixta to kiss him. She turned her face, that was almost ugly after the night's dissipation, and looked steadily into his.

"I don' want to kiss you, Bobinôt," she said, turning away again, "not to-day. Some other time. *Bonté divine!* ent you satisfy, *yet*!"

"Oh, I'm satisfy, Calixta," he said.

Riding through a patch of wood, Clarisse's saddle became ungirted, and she and Alcée dismounted to readjust it.

For the twentieth time he asked her what had happened at home.

"But, Clarisse, w'at is it? Is it a misfortune?"

"Ah Dieu sait! It's only something that happen' to me."

"To you!"

"I saw you go away las' night, Alcée, with those saddle-bags," she said, haltingly, striving to arrange something about the saddle, "an' I made Bruce tell me. He said you had gone to the ball, an' wouldn' be home for weeks an' weeks. I thought, Alcée—maybe you were going to—to Assumption. I got wild. An' then I knew if you did n't come back, *now*, to-night, I could n't stan' it,—again."

She had her face hidden in her arm that she was resting against the saddle when she said that.

He began to wonder if this meant love. But she had to tell him so, before he believed it. And when she told him, he thought the face of the Universe was changed—just like Bobinôt. Was it last week the cyclone had well-nigh ruined him? The cyclone seemed a huge joke, now. It was he, then, who, an hour ago was kissing little Calixta's ear and whispering nonsense into it. Calixta was like a myth, now. The one, only, great reality in the world was Clarisse standing before him, telling him that she loved him.

In the distance they heard the rapid discharge of pistol-shots; but it did not disturb them. They knew it was only the negro musicians who had gone into the yard to fire their pistols into the air, as the custom is, and to announce "*le bal est fini.*"

LA BELLE ZORAÏDE

The summer night was hot and still; not a ripple of air swept over the marais. Yonder, across Bayou St. John, lights twinkled here and there in the darkness, and in the dark sky above a few stars were blinking. A lugger that had come out of the lake was moving with slow, lazy motion down the bayou. A man in the boat was singing a song.

The notes of the song came faintly to the ears of old Manna Loulou, herself as black as the night, who had gone out upon the gallery to open the shutters wide.

Something in the refrain reminded the woman of an old, half-forgotten Creole romance, and she began to sing it low to herself while she threw the shutters open:—

> *"Lisett' to kité la plaine,*
> *Mo perdi bonhair à moué;*
> *Ziés à moué semblé fontaine,*
> *Dépi mo pa miré toué."*

And then this old song, a lover's lament for the loss of his mistress, floating into her memory, brought with it the story she would tell to Madame, who lay in her sumptuous mahogany bed, waiting to be fanned and put to sleep to the sound of one of Manna Loulou's stories. The old negress had already bathed her mistress's pretty white feet and kissed them lovingly, one, then the other. She had brushed her mistress's beautiful hair, that was as soft and shining as satin, and was the color of Madame's wedding-ring. Now, when she reëntered the room, she moved softly toward the bed, and seating herself there began gently to fan Madame Delisle.

Manna Loulou was not always ready with her story, for Madame would hear none but those which were true. But to-night the story was all there in Manna Loulou's head—the story of la belle Zoraïde—and she told it to her mistress in the soft Creole patois, whose music and charm no English words can convey.

La belle Zoraïde had eyes that were so dusky, so beautiful, that any man who gazed too long into their depths was sure to lose his head, and even his heart sometimes. Her soft, smooth skin was the color of *café-au-lait*.

As for her elegant manners, her *svelte* and graceful figure, they were the envy of half the ladies who visited her mistress, Madame Delarivière.

"No wonder Zoraïde was as charming and as dainty as the finest lady of la rue Royale: from a toddling thing she had been brought up at her mistress's side; her fingers had never done rougher work than sewing a fine muslin seam; and she even had her own little black servant to wait upon her. Madame, who was her godmother as well as her mistress, would often say to her:—

"'Remember, Zoraïde, when you are ready to marry, it must be in a way to do honor to your bringing up. It will be at the Cathedral. Your wedding gown, your corbeille, all will be of the best; I shall see to that myself. You know, M'sieur Ambroise is ready whenever you say the word; and his master is willing to do as much for him as I shall do for you. It is a union that will please me in every way.'

"M'sieur Ambroise was then the body servant of Doctor Langlé. La belle Zoraïde detested the little mulatto, with his shining whiskers like a white man's, and his small eyes, that were cruel and false as a snake's. She would cast down her own mischievous eyes, and say:—

"'Ah, nénaine, I am so happy, so contented here at your side just as I am. I don't want to marry now; next year, perhaps, or the next.' And Madame would smile indulgently and remind Zoraïde that a woman's charms are not everlasting.

"But the truth of the matter was, Zoraïde had seen le beau Mézor dance the Bamboula in Congo Square. That was a sight to hold one rooted to the ground. Mézor was as straight as a cypress-tree and as proud looking as a king. His body, bare to the waist, was like a column of ebony and it glistened like oil.

"Poor Zoraïde's heart grew sick in her bosom with love for le beau Mézor from the moment she saw the fierce gleam of his eye, lighted by the inspiring strains of the Bamboula, and beheld the stately movements of his splendid body swaying and quivering through the figures of the dance.

"But when she knew him later, and he came near her to speak with her, all the fierceness was gone out of his eyes, and she saw only kindness in them and heard only gentleness in his voice; for love had taken possession of him also, and Zoraïde was more distracted than ever. When Mézor was not dancing Bamboula in Congo Square, he was hoeing sugar-cane, barefooted and half naked, in his master's field outside of the city. Doctor Langlé was his master as well as M'sieur Ambroise's.

"One day, when Zoraïde kneeled before her mistress, drawing on Madame's silken stockings, that were of the finest, she said: "'Nénaine, you have spoken to me often of marrying. Now, at last, I have chosen a husband, but it is not M'sieur Ambroise; it is le beau Mézor that I want and no other.' And Zoraïde hid her face in her hands when she had said that, for she guessed, rightly enough, that her mistress would be very angry. And, indeed, Madame Delarivière was at first speechless with rage. When she finally spoke it was only to gasp out, exasperated:—

"'That negro! that negro! Bon Dieu Seigneur, but this is too much!'

"'Am I white, nénaine?' pleaded Zoraïde.

"'You white! *Malheureuse!* You deserve to have the lash laid upon you like any other slave; you have proven yourself no better than the worst.'

"'I am not white,' persisted Zoraïde, respectfully and gently. 'Doctor Langlé gives me his slave to marry, but he would not give me his son. Then, since I am not white, let me have from out of my own race the one whom my heart has chosen.'

"However, you may well believe that Madame would not hear to that. Zoraïde was forbidden to speak to Mézor, and Mézor was cautioned against seeing Zoraïde again. But you know how the negroes are, Ma'zélle Titite," added Manna Loulou, smiling a little sadly. "There is no mistress, no master, no king nor priest who can hinder them from loving when they will. And these two found ways and means.

"When months had passed by, Zoraïde, who had grown unlike herself,—sober and preoccupied,—said again to her mistress:—

"'Nénaine, you would not let me have Mézor for my husband; but I have disobeyed you, I have sinned. Kill me if you wish, nénaine: forgive me if you will; but when I heard le beau Mézor say to me, "Zoraïde, mo l'aime toi," I could have died, but I could not have helped loving him.'

"This time Madame Delarivière was so actually pained, so wounded at hearing Zoraïde's confession, that there was no place left in her heart for anger. She could utter only confused reproaches. But she was a woman of action rather than of words, and she acted promptly. Her first step was to induce Doctor Langlé to sell Mézor. Doctor Langlé, who was a widower, had long wanted to marry Madame Delarivière, and he would willingly have walked on all fours at noon through the Place d'Armes if she wanted him to. Naturally he lost no time in disposing of le beau Mézor, who was sold away into Georgia, or the Carolinas, or one of those distant countries far away, where he would no longer hear his Creole tongue spoken, nor dance Calinda, nor hold la belle Zoraïde in his arms.

"The poor thing was heartbroken when Mézor was sent away from her, but she took comfort and hope in the thought of her baby that she would soon be able to clasp to her breast.

"La belle Zoraïde's sorrows had now begun in earnest. Not only sorrows but sufferings, and with the anguish of maternity came the shadow of death. But there is no agony that a mother will not forget when she holds her first-born to her heart, and presses her lips upon the baby flesh that is her own, yet far more precious than her own.

"So, instinctively, when Zoraïde came out of the awful shadow she gazed questioningly about her and felt with her trembling hands upon either side of her. 'Où li, mo piti a moin? where is my little one?' she asked imploringly. Madame who was there and the nurse who was there both told her in turn, 'To piti à toi, li mouri' ('Your little one is dead'), which was a wicked falsehood that must have caused the angels in heaven to weep. For the baby was living and well and strong. It had at once been removed from its mother's side, to be sent away to Madame's plantation, far up the coast. Zoraïde could only moan in reply, 'Li mouri, li mouri,' and she turned her face to the wall.

"Madame had hoped, in thus depriving Zoraïde of her child, to have her young waiting-maid again at her side free, happy, and beautiful as of old. But there was a more powerful will than Madame's at work—the will of the good God, who had already designed that Zoraïde should grieve with a sorrow that was never more to be lifted in this world. La belle Zoraïde was no more. In her stead was a sad-eyed woman who mourned night and day for her baby. 'Li mouri, li mouri,' she would sigh over and over again to those about her, and to herself when others grew weary of her complaint.

"Yet, in spite of all, M'sieur Ambroise was still in the notion to marry her. A sad wife or a merry one was all the same to him so long as that wife was Zoraïde. And she seemed to consent, or rather submit, to the approaching marriage as though nothing mattered any longer in this world.

"One day, a black servant entered a little noisily the room in which Zoraïde sat sewing. With a look of strange and vacuous happiness upon her face, Zoraïde arose hastily. 'Hush, hush,' she whispered, lifting a warning finger, 'my little one is asleep; you must not awaken her.'

"Upon the bed was a senseless bundle of rags shaped like an infant in swaddling clothes. Over this dummy the woman had drawn the mosquito bar, and she was sitting contentedly beside it. In short, from that day Zoraïde was demented. Night nor day did she lose sight of the doll that lay in her bed or in her arms.

"And now was Madame stung with sorrow and remorse at seeing this terrible affliction that had befallen her dear Zoraïde. Consulting with Doctor Langlé, they decided to bring back to the mother the real baby of flesh and blood that was now toddling about, and kicking its heels in the dust yonder upon the plantation.

"It was Madame herself who led the pretty, tiny little "griffe" girl to her mother. Zoraïde was sitting upon a stone bench in the courtyard, listening to the soft splashing of the fountain, and watching the fitful shadows of the palm leaves upon the broad, white flagging.

"'Here,' said Madame, approaching, 'here, my poor dear Zoraïde, is your own little child. Keep her; she is yours. No one will ever take her from you again.'

"Zoraïde looked with sullen suspicion upon her mistress and the child before her. Reaching out a hand she thrust the little one mistrustfully away from her. With the other hand she clasped the rag bundle fiercely to her breast; for she suspected a plot to deprive her of it.

"Nor could she ever be induced to let her own child approach her; and finally the little one was sent back to the plantation, where she was never to know the love of mother or father.

"And now this is the end of Zoraïde's story. She was never known again as la belle Zoraïde, but ever after as Zoraïde la folle, whom no one ever wanted to marry—not even M'sieur Ambroise. She lived to be an old woman, whom some people pitied and others laughed at—always clasping her bundle of rags—her 'piti.'

"Are you asleep, Ma'zélle Titite?"

"No, I am not asleep; I was thinking. Ah, the poor little one, Man Loulou, the poor little one! better had she died!"

But this is the way Madame Delisle and Manna Loulou really talked to each other:—

"Vou pré droumi, Ma'zélle Titite?"

"Non, pa pré droumi; mo yapré zongler. Ah, la pauv' piti, Man Loulou. La pauv' piti! Mieux li mouri!"

A Gentleman of Bayou Têche

It was no wonder Mr. Sublet, who was staying at the Hallet plantation, wanted to make a picture of Evariste. The 'Cadian was rather a picturesque subject in his way, and a tempting one to an artist looking for bits of "local color" along the Têche.

Mr. Sublet had seen the man on the back gallery just as he came out of the swamp, trying to sell a wild turkey to the house-keeper. He spoke to him at once, and in the course of conversation engaged him to return to the house the following morning and have his picture drawn. He handed Evariste a couple of silver dollars to show that his intentions were fair, and that he expected the 'Cadian to keep faith with him.

"He tell' me he want' put my picture in one fine '*Mag*'zine,'" said Evariste to his daughter, Martinette, when the two were talking the matter over in the afternoon.

"W'at fo' you reckon he want' do dat?" They sat within the low, homely cabin of two rooms, that was not quite so comfortable as Mr. Hallet's negro quarters.

Martinette pursed her red lips that had little sensitive curves to them, and her black eyes took on a reflective expression.

"Mebbe he yeard 'bout that big fish w'at you ketch las' winta in Carancro lake. You know it was all wrote about in the 'Suga Bowl.'" Her father set aside the suggestion with a deprecatory wave of the hand.

"Well, anyway, you got to fix yo'se'f up," declared Martinette, dismissing further speculation; "put on yo' otha pant'loon' an' yo' good coat; an' you betta ax Mr. Léonce to cut yo' hair, an' yo' w'sker' a li'le bit."

"It's w'at I say," chimed in Evariste. "I tell dat gent'man I'm goin' make myse'f fine. He say', 'No, no,' like he ent please'. He want' me like I come out de swamp. So much betta if my pant'loon' an' coat is tore, he-say, an' color' like de mud." They could not understand these eccentric wishes on the part of the strange gentleman, and made no effort to do so.

An hour later Martinette, who was quite puffed up over the affair, trotted across to Aunt Dicey's cabin to communicate the news to her. The negress was ironing; her irons stood in a long row before the fire of logs that burned on the hearth. Martinette seated herself in the chimney corner and held her feet up to the blaze; it was damp and a little chilly out of doors. The girl's shoes were considerably worn and her garments were a little too thin and scant for the winter season. Her father had given her the two dollars he had received from the artist, and Martinette was on her way to the store to invest them as judiciously as she knew how.

"You know, Aunt Dicey," she began a little complacently after listening awhile to Aunt Dicey's unqualified abuse of her own son, Wilkins, who was dining-room boy at Mr. Hallet's, "you know that stranger gentleman up to Mr. Hallet's? he want' to make my popa's picture; an' he say' he goin' put it in one fine Mag'zine yonda." Aunt Dicey spat upon her iron to test its heat. Then she began to snicker. She kept on laughing inwardly, making her whole fat body shake, and saying nothing.

"W'at you laughin' 'bout, Aunt Dice?" inquired Martinette mistrustfully.

"I is n' laughin', chile!"

"Yas, you' laughin'."

"Oh, don't pay no 'tention to me. I jis studyin' how simple you an' yo' pa is. You is bof de simplest somebody I eva come 'crost."

"You got to say plumb out w'at you mean, Aunt Dice," insisted the girl doggedly, suspicious and alert now.

"Well, dat w'y I say you is simple," proclaimed the woman, slamming down her iron on an inverted, battered pie pan, "jis like you says, dey gwine put yo' pa's picture yonda in de picture paper. An' you know w'at readin' dey gwine sot down on'neaf dat picture?" Martinette was intensely attentive. "Dey gwine sot down on'neaf: 'Dis heah is one dem low-down 'Cajuns o' Bayeh Têche!'"

The blood flowed from Martinette's face, leaving it deathly pale; in another instant it came beating back in a quick flood, and her eyes smarted with pain as if the tears that filled them had been fiery hot.

"I knows dem kine o' folks," continued Aunt Dicey, resuming her interrupted ironing. "Dat stranger he got a li'le boy w'at ain't none too big to spank. Dat li'le imp he come a hoppin' in heah yistiddy wid a kine o' box on'neaf his arm. He say' 'Good mo'nin', madam. Will you be so kine an' stan' jis like you is dah at yo' i'onin', an' lef me take yo' picture?' I 'lowed I gwine make a picture outen him wid dis heah flat-i'on, ef he don' d'ar hisse'f quick. An' he say he baig my pardon fo' his intrudement. All dat kine o' talk to a ole nigga 'oman! Dat plainly sho' he don' know his place."

"W'at you want 'im to say, Aunt Dice?" asked Martinette, with an effort to conceal her distress.

"I wants 'im to come in heah an' say: 'Howdy, Aunt Dicey! will you be so kine and go put on yo' noo calker dress an' yo' bonnit w'at you w'ars to meetin', an' stan' 'side f'om dat i'onin'-boa'd w'ilse I gwine take yo' photgraph.' Dat de way fo' a boy to talk w'at had good raisin'."

Martinette had arisen, and began to take slow leave of the woman. She turned at the cabin door to observe tentatively: "I reckon it's Wilkins tells you how the folks they talk, yonda up to Mr. Hallet's."

She did not go to the store as she had intended, but walked with a dragging step back to her home. The silver dollars clicked in her pocket as she walked. She felt like flinging them across the field; they seemed to her somehow the price of shame.

The sun had sunk, and twilight was settling like a silver beam upon the bayou and enveloping the fields in a gray mist. Evariste, slim and slouchy, was waiting for his daughter in the cabin door. He had lighted a fire of sticks and branches, and placed the kettle before it to boil. He met the girl with his slow, serious, questioning eyes, astonished to see her empty-handed.

"How come you didn' bring nuttin' f'om de sto', Martinette?"

She entered and flung her gingham sun-bonnet upon a chair. "No, I didn' go yonda;" and with sudden exasperation: "You got to go take back that money; you mus' n' git no picture took."

"But, Martinette," her father mildly interposed, "I promise' 'im; an' he's goin' give me some mo' money w'en he finish."

"If he give you a ba'el o' money, you mus' n' git no picture took. You know w'at he want to put un'neath that picture, fo' ev'body to read?" She could not tell him the whole hideous truth as she had heard it distorted from Aunt Dicey's lips; she would not hurt him that much. "He's goin' to write: 'This is one *Cajun* o' the Bayou Têche.'" Evariste winced.

"How you know?" he asked.

"I yeard so. I know it's true."

The water in the kettle was boiling. He went and poured a small quantity upon the coffee which he had set there to drip. Then he said to her: "I reckon you jus' as well go care dat two dolla' back, tomo' mo'nin'; me, I'll go yonda ketch a mess o' fish in Carancro lake."

MR. HALLET AND A FEW MASCULINE companions were assembled at a rather late breakfast the following morning. The dining-room was a big, bare one, enlivened by a cheerful fire of logs that blazed in the wide chimney on massive andirons. There were guns, fishing tackle, and other implements of sport lying about. A couple of fine dogs strayed unceremoniously in and out behind Wilkins, the negro boy who waited upon the table. The chair beside Mr. Sublet, usually occupied by his little son, was vacant, as the child had gone for an early morning outing and had not yet returned.

When breakfast was about half over, Mr. Hallet noticed Martinette standing outside upon the gallery. The dining-room door had stood open more than half the time.

"Isn't that Martinette out there, Wilkins" inquired the jovial-faced young planter.

"Dat's who, suh," returned Wilkins. "She ben standin' dah sence mos' sun-up; look like she studyin' to take root to de gall'ry."

"What in the name of goodness does she want? Ask her what she wants. Tell her to come in to the fire."

Martinette walked into the room with much hesitancy. Her small, brown face could hardly be seen in the depths of the gingham sun-bonnet. Her blue cottonade skirt scarcely, reached the thin ankles that it should have covered.

"Bonjou'," she murmured, with a little comprehensive nod that took in the entire company. Her eyes searched the table for the "stranger gentleman," and she knew him at once, because his hair was parted in the middle and he wore a pointed beard. She went and laid the two silver dollars beside his plate and motioned to retire without a word of explanation.

"Hold on, Martinette!" called out the planter, "what's all this pantomime business? Speak out, little one."

"My popa don't want any picture took," she offered, a little timorously. On her way to the door she had looked back to say this. In that fleeting glance she detected a smile of intelligence pass from one to the other of the group. She turned quickly, facing them all, and spoke out, excitement making her voice bold and shrill: "My popa ent one low-down 'Cajun. He ent goin' to stan' to have that kine o' writin' put down un'neath his picture!"

She almost ran from the room, half blinded by the emotion that had helped her to make so daring a speech.

Descending the gallery steps she ran full against her father who was ascending, bearing in his arms the little boy, Archie Sublet. The child was most grotesquely attired in garments far too large for his diminutive person—the rough jeans clothing of some negro boy. Evariste himself had evidently been taking a bath without the preliminary ceremony of removing his clothes, that were now half dried upon his person by the wind and sun.

"Yere you' li'le boy," he announced, stumbling into the room. "You ought not lef dat li'le chile go by hisse'f *comme ça* in de pirogue." Mr. Sublet darted from his chair; the others following suit almost as hastily. In an instant, quivering with apprehension, he had his little son in his arms. The child was quite unharmed, only somewhat pale and nervous, as the consequence of a recent very serious ducking.

Evariste related in his uncertain, broken English how he had been fishing for an hour or more in Carancro lake, when he noticed the boy paddling over the deep, black water in a shell-like pirogue. Nearing a clump of cypress-trees that rose from the lake, the pirogue became entangled in the heavy moss that hung from the tree limbs and trailed upon the water. The next thing he knew, the boat had overturned, he heard the child scream, and saw him disappear beneath the still, black surface of the lake.

"W'en I done swim to de sho' wid 'im," continued Evariste, "I hurry yonda to Jake Baptiste's cabin, an' we rub 'im an' warm 'im up, an' dress 'im up dry like you see. He all right now, M'sieur; but you mus'n lef 'im go no mo' by hisse'f in one pirogue."

Martinette had followed into the room behind her father. She was feeling and tapping his wet garments solicitously, and begging him in French to come home. Mr. Hallet at once ordered hot coffee and a warm breakfast for the two; and they sat down at the corner of the table, making no manner of objection in their perfect simplicity. It was with visible reluctance and ill-disguised contempt that Wilkins served them.

When Mr. Sublet had arranged his son comfortably, with tender care, upon the sofa, and had satisfied himself that the child was quite uninjured, he attempted to find words with which to thank Evariste for this service which no treasure of words or gold could pay for. These warm and heartfelt expressions seemed to Evariste to exaggerate the importance of his action, and they intimidated him. He attempted shyly to hide his face as well as he could in the depths of his bowl of coffee.

"You will let me make your picture now, I hope, Evariste," begged Mr. Sublet, laying his hand upon the 'Cadian's shoulder. "I want to place it among things I hold most dear, and shall call it 'A hero of Bayou Têche.'" This assurance seemed to distress Evariste greatly.

"No, no," he protested, "it's nuttin' hero' to take a li'le boy out de water. I jus' as easy do dat like I stoop down an' pick up a li'le chile w'at fall down in de road. I ent goin' to 'low dat, me. I don't git no picture took, *va!*"

Mr. Hallet, who now discerned his friend's eagerness in the matter, came to his aid.

"I tell you, Evariste, let Mr. Sublet draw your picture, and you yourself may call it whatever you want. I'm sure he 'll let you."

"Most willingly," agreed the artist.

Evariste glanced up at him with shy and child-like pleasure. "It's a bargain?" he asked.

"A bargain," affirmed Mr. Sublet.

"Popa," whispered Martinette, "you betta come-home an' put on yo' otha pant'loon' an' yo' good coat."

"And now, what shall we call the much talked-of picture?" cheerily inquired the planter, standing with his back to the blaze.

Evariste in a business-like manner began carefully to trace on the tablecloth imaginary characters with an imaginary pen; he could not have written the real characters with a real pen—he did not know how.

"You will put on'neat' de picture," he said, deliberately, "'Dis is one picture of Mista Evariste Anatole Bonamour, a gent'man of de Bayou Têche.'"

A Lady of Bayou St. John

The days and the nights were very lonely for Madame Delisle. Gustave, her husband, was away yonder in Virginia somewhere, with Beauregard, and she was here in the old house on Bayou St. John, alone with her slaves.

Madame was very beautiful. So beautiful, that she found much diversion in sitting for hours before the mirror, contemplating her own loveliness; admiring the brilliancy of her golden hair, the sweet languor of her blue eyes, the graceful contours of her figure, and the peach-like bloom of her flesh. She was very young. So young that she romped with the dogs, teased the parrot, and could not fall asleep at night unless old black Manna-Loulou sat beside her bed and told her stories.

In short, she was a child, not able to realize the significance of the tragedy whose unfolding kept the civilized world in suspense. It was only the immediate effect of the awful drama that moved her: the gloom that, spreading on all sides, penetrated her own existence and deprived it of joyousness.

Sépincourt found her looking very lonely and disconsolate one day when he stopped to talk with her. She was pale, and her blue eyes were dim with unwept tears. He was a Frenchman who lived near by. He shrugged his shoulders over this strife between brothers, this quarrel which was none of his; and he resented it chiefly upon the ground that it made life uncomfortable; yet he was young enough to have had quicker and hotter blood in his veins.

When he left Madame Delisle that day, her eyes were no longer dim, and a something of the dreariness that weighted her had been lifted away. That mysterious, that treacherous bond called sympathy, had revealed them to each other.

He came to her very often that summer, clad always in cool, white duck, with a flower in his buttonhole. His pleasant brown eyes sought hers with warm, friendly glances that comforted her as a caress might comfort a disconsolate child. She took to watching for his slim figure, a little bent, walking lazily up the avenue between the double line of magnolias.

They would sit sometimes during whole afternoons in the vine-sheltered corner of the gallery, sipping the black coffee that Manna-Loulou brought to them at intervals; and talking, talking incessantly during the first days when they were unconsciously unfolding themselves to each other. Then a time came—it came very quickly—when they seemed to have nothing more to say to one another.

He brought her news of the war; and they talked about it listlessly, between long intervals of silence, of which neither took account. An occasional letter came by round-about ways from Gustave—guarded arid saddening in its tone. They would read it and sigh over it together.

Once they stood before his portrait that hung in the drawing-room and that looked out at them with kind, indulgent eyes. Madame wiped the picture with her gossamer handkerchief and impulsively pressed a tender kiss upon the painted canvas. For months past the living image of her husband had been receding further and further into a mist which she could penetrate with no faculty or power that she possessed.

One day at sunset, when she and Sépincourt stood silently side by side, looking across the *marais*, aflame with the western light, he said to her: "*M'amie*, let us go away from this country that is so *triste*. Let us go to Paris, you and me."

She thought that he was jesting, and she laughed nervously. "Yes, Paris would surely be gayer than Bayou St. John," she answered. But he was not jesting. She saw it at once in the glance that penetrated her own; in the quiver of his sensitive lip and the quick beating of a swollen vein in his brown throat.

"Paris, or anywhere—with you—ah, *bon Dieu!*" he whispered, seizing her hands. But she withdrew from him, frightened, and hurried away into the house, leaving him alone.

That night, for the first time, Madame did not want to hear Manna-Loulou's stories, and she blew out the wax candle that till now had burned nightly, in her sleeping-room, under its tall, crystal globe. She had suddenly become a woman capable of love or sacrifice. She would not hear Manna-Loulou's stories. She wanted to be alone, to tremble and to weep.

In the morning her eyes were dry, but she would not see Sépincourt when he came. Then he wrote her a letter.

"I have offended you and I would rather die!" it ran. "Do not banish me from your presence that is life to me. Let me lie at your feet, if only for a moment, in which to hear you say that you forgive me."

Men have written just such letters before, but Madame did not know it. To her it was a voice from the unknown, like music, awaking in her a delicious tumult that seized and held possession of her whole being.

When they met, he had but to look into her face to know that he need not lie at her feet craving forgiveness. She was waiting for him beneath the spreading branches of a live-oak that guarded the gate of her home like a sentinel.

For a brief moment he held her hands, which trembled. Then he folded her in his arms and kissed her many times. "You will go with me, *m'amie*? I love you—oh, I love you! Will you not go with me, *m'amie*?"

"Anywhere, anywhere," she told him in a fainting voice that he could scarcely hear.

But she did not go with him. Chance willed it otherwise. That night a courier brought her a message from Beauregard, telling her that Gustave, her husband, was dead.

When the new year was still young, Sépincourt decided that, all things considered, he might, without any appearance of indecent haste, speak again of his love to Madame Delisle. That love was quite as acute as ever; perhaps a little sharper, from the long period of silence and waiting to which he had subjected it. He found her, as he had expected, clad in deepest mourning. She greeted him precisely as she had welcomed the curé, when the kind old priest had brought to her the consolations of religion—clasping his two hands warmly, and calling him "cher ami." Her whole attitude and bearing brought to Sépincourt the poignant, the bewildering conviction that he held no place in her thoughts.

They sat in the drawing-room before the portrait of Gustave, which was draped with his scarf. Above the picture hung his sword, and beneath it was an embankment of flowers. Sépincourt felt an almost irresistible impulse to bend his knee before this altar, upon which he saw foreshadowed the immolation of his hopes.

There was a soft air blowing gently over the *marais*. It came to them through the open window, laden with a hundred subtle sounds and scents of the springtime. It seemed to remind Madame of something far, far away, for she gazed dreamily out into the blue firmament. It fretted Sépincourt with impulses to speech and action which he found it impossible to control.

"You must know what has brought me," he began impulsively, drawing his chair nearer to hers. "Through all these months I have never ceased to love you and to long for you. Night and day the sound of your dear voice has been with me; your eyes"—She held out her hand deprecatingly. He took it and held it. She let it lie unresponsive in his.

"You cannot have forgotten that you loved me not long ago," he went on eagerly, "that you were ready to follow me anywhere,—anywhere; do you remember? I have come now to ask you to fulfill that promise; to ask you toy be my wife, my companion, the dear treasure of my life."

She heard his warm and pleading tones as though listening to a strange language, imperfectly understood.

She withdrew her hand from his, and leaned her brow thoughtfully upon it.

"Can you not feel—can you not understand, *mon ami*," she said calmly, "that now such a thing—such a thought, is impossible to me?"

"Impossible?"

"Yes, impossible. Can you not see that now my heart, my soul, my thought—my very life, must belong to another? It could not be different."

"Would you have me believe that you can wed your young existence to the dead?" he exclaimed with something like horror. Her glance was sunk deep in the embankment of flowers before her.

"My husband has never been so living to me as he is now," she replied with a faint smile of commiseration for Sépincourt's fatuity. "Every object that surrounds me speaks to me of him. I look yonder across the *marais*, and I see him coming toward me, tired and toil-stained from the hunt. I see him again sitting in this chair or in that one. I hear his familiar voice, his footsteps upon the galleries. We walk once more together beneath the magnolias; and at night in dreams I feel that he is there, there, near me. How could it be different! Ah! I have memories, memories to crowd and fill my life, if I live a hundred years!"

Sépincourt was wondering why she did not take the sword down from her altar and thrust it through his body here and there. The effect would have been infinitely more agreeable than her words, penetrating his soul like fire. He arose confused, enraged with pain.

"Then, Madame," he stammered, "there is nothing left for me but to take my leave. I bid you adieu."

"Do not be offended, *mon ami*," she said kindly, holding out her hand. "You are going to Paris, I suppose?"

"What does it matter," he exclaimed desperately, "where I go?"

"Oh, I only wanted to wish you *bon voyage*" she assured him amiably.

Many days after that Sépincourt spent in the fruitless mental effort of trying to comprehend that psychological enigma, a woman's heart.

Madame still lives on Bayou St. John. She is rather an old lady now, a very pretty old lady, against whose long years of widowhood there has never been a breath of reproach. The memory of Gustave still fills and satisfies her days. She has never failed, once a year, to have a solemn high mass said for the repose of his soul.

A Note About the Author

Kate Chopin (1850–1904) was an American writer. Born in St. Louis, Missouri to a family with French and Irish ancestry, Chopin was raised Roman Catholic. An avid reader, Chopin graduated from Sacred Heart Convent in 1968 before marrying Oscar Chopin, with whom she moved to New Orleans in 1870. The two had six children before Oscar's death in 1882, which left the family with extensive debts and forced Kate to take over her husband's businesses, including the management of several plantations and a general store. In the early 1890s, back in St. Louis and suffering from depression, Chopin began writing short stories, articles, and translations for local newspapers and literary magazines. Although she achieved moderate critical acclaim for her second novel, *The Awakening* (1899)—now considered a classic of American literature and a pioneering work of feminist fiction—fame and success eluded her in her lifetime. In the years since her death, however, Chopin has been recognized as a leading author of her generation who captured with a visionary intensity the lives of Southern women, often of diverse or indeterminate racial background.

A Note from the Publisher

Spanning many genres, from non-fiction essays to literature classics to children's books and lyric poetry, Mint Edition books showcase the master works of our time in a modern new package. The text is freshly typeset, is clean and easy to read, and features a new note about the author in each volume. Many books also include exclusive new introductory material. Every book boasts a striking new cover, which makes it as appropriate for collecting as it is for gift giving. Mint Edition books are only printed when a reader orders them, so natural resources are not wasted. We're proud that our books are never manufactured in excess and exist only in the exact quantity they need to be read and enjoyed.

Discover more of your favorite classics with Bookfinity™.

- Track your reading with custom book lists.
- Get great book recommendations for your personalized Reader Type.
- Add reviews for your favorite books.
- AND MUCH MORE!

Visit **bookfinity.com** and take the fun Reader Type quiz to get started.

Enjoy our classic and modern companion pairings!

Printed in the USA
CPSIA information can be obtained
at www.ICGtesting.com
JSHW082346140824
68134JS00020B/1915

9 781513 271620